Praise and Awards for *Pharmacy Girl:*

The Great War, Spanish Influenza, and the Truth About Billy Detwiler

2020 National Federation of Press Women 2nd Place Award for Children's Fiction

2020 Delaware Press Association Award for Children's Fiction

2019 Moonbeam Children's Fiction Silver Medal for Pre-teen Historical/Cultural Fiction

⌘

I liked *Pharmacy Girl* because it describes every day in the lives of kids from a long time ago.

Charlie, grade 5

A good amount of action, and just enough sadness and death. She did really well at making the reader love characters like Josie, Grace, Tiny, Gram, and Ms. Penny, and hate characters like Billy Detwiler, Mrs. Detwiler, and the Mackenzie brothers, and the Kaiser. Overall an awesome book!

Hannah, grade 6

I loved it!

Lillian, grade 6

The spunky, likeable heroine, Josie, shows us her world and makes us want to root for her and her family from beginning to end. Upper elementary and middle schoolers should enjoy this book and find it hard to put down!

Jill Flynn, Professor of English

Pharmacy Girl **should win an award....** *Pharmacy Girl* transports you to 1918 in scenes that are alternately funny, interesting, exciting, devastating, and poignant. This historical fiction is fresh, with a strong heroine who is as charming and compelling as any modern-day protagonist. It will capture your heart!

Susan Robinson, author and editor

Szegda has surrounded Josie with an appealing cast of supporting characters, creating well-drawn and realistic moments for Josie's troublesome sister Clementine, her supportive parents, her sensible friend Grace, and even bully Billy Detwiler. A brave girl who wants to do her part, Josie is a heroine that readers will cheer on to the climactic and satisfying moment of crisis when she shows both her resilience and her character.

Loretta Carlson, freelance writer and editor

A compelling read, this novel is grounded in history and propelled by the adventures of likable -and unlikable - characters. I don't know who enjoyed the book more, my grandchildren or me!

Linda Emerick, retired middle school ELA teacher

The book gives a glimpse into what family life was like during a time when WW1 was still raging, the influenza epidemic was spreading, and not much was known about the science regarding infectious disease. The description of the drug store brought much nostalgia to me as a similar pharmacy was where my high school friends and I would hang out by the soda fountain.

Randall Reid, retired R.N., pharmaceutical professional

Pharmacy Girl **gives insight into what was going on in a New Jersey town in 1918 ….** The characters' actions mirrored the events of that time and displayed how a loving family coped in their small community. I enjoyed this first offering from Kate Szegda and hope to read more in the future.

Linda Jemmett, retired school librarian

As people she knows and loves sicken and die, Josie keeps trying to do the right thing. Keeps trying to be a person you can count on, the way her father, the town pharmacist, has always been. But sometimes "the right thing" isn't so easy to figure out, and it's even harder to do.

Carolyn Griffith, freelance writer

PHARMACY GIRL

The Great War, Spanish Influenza, and
the Truth About Billy Detwiler

KATE SZEGDA

ISBN: 9781791660574

Back cover photo used with permission from the University of Delaware.

www.happyselfpublisher.com

For my mother and her sister who told me the stories
from the pharmacy

TABLE OF CONTENTS

Exposure

A Nation Comes Down with the Flu

Crisis

Resolution

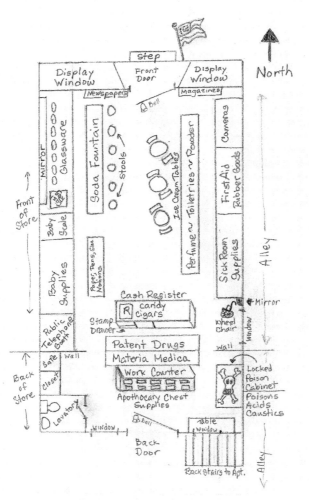

North

My Favorite Place
Winslow's Drug Store

J. Winslow
Sept. 3, 1918

CHAPTER ONE

THE GUN

August 31, 1918
Highland Park, New Jersey

"Good morning. Winslow's Drug Store. Josie speaking . . . Yes, I'll tell them . . . I love you too." I hung up the telephone. "That was Gram," I told my parents. "She needs to stay an extra hour to finish packing care packages for the soldiers."

Grace and I had made plans to go to the library—our usual Saturday excursion—and I hoped Gram's delay wouldn't mean we'd have to cancel them. I couldn't wait to check out the next Ruth Fielding novel. And Grace and I needed to finalize our places for the Labor Day parade. All these years of watching parades, and now we were going to be in one! I felt a shiver of excitement. For now, though, it was store chores and babysitting my four-year-old sister.

Dad was putting up prescriptions in the pharmacy, and I knew better than to disturb him. Distractions could mean a mistake. And a mistake could be deadly. Mother was busy with Mrs. Johnson, who'd brought her baby in to be weighed. But first there was a lot of "ga-ga-goo-goo" and fussing over the infant. Through the screen doors I could hear a late-August locust buzzing outside, a sure sign it would be hot all day.

"Can we have something to drink?" Tiny asked.

"Let's finish this last bit of dusting, and then maybe we can have lemonade," I said, climbing onto the step stool to dust the eight-foot-high shelves that separated the pharmacy from the front of the store.

Cardboard containers crashed to the floor and I heard a little "uh-oh" from Tiny. Fiddlesticks. I climbed back down and helped Tiny put the fallen merchandise back in place.

"Can we have ice cream?" Tiny asked.

I shook my head. "I thought you wanted a drink."

"Ice cream. It's colder."

There was a chuckle from the pharmacy. I looked up to see Dad in the mirror he had rigged in the doorway. The mirror let him see the cash register while he was working in the back of the store. Dad was trying not to laugh at Tiny. "Clementine, you know the rule. No treats until you finish."

"See," I said. "We're almost done. All we have left to do is the penny candy case."

"Can I have a Mary Jane?" Tiny asked.

"Now you want candy? You just said you wanted ice cream."

"Where's Grandma? She lets me have treats."

"Grandma's helping the Red Cross pack *treats* for the *soldiers.*"

The front screen door banged open and Mrs. Johnson's baby wailed.

Oh no. It was Billy Detwiler *and* his mother. I wanted to cry too. Mrs. Detwiler was mean, and she acted as if she were the Queen of Sheba, expecting everyone to stop and do her bidding.

"I need stamps today, Ethel," Mrs. Detwiler announced as she promenaded through the store. "We're in a hurry. I'm taking Billy over to Reed's Book Store for school supplies, and we don't want to miss the trolley."

Mother was polite. "I'm almost done with Mrs. Johnson, and then I will be right with you," she said over the crying infant.

"Well." Mrs. Detwiler stuck out her chin and gave a little harrumph. "The trolley will be here any moment."

Trolleys ran past our store every half hour. I glanced at the huge regulator clock on the back wall. It was 11:10. She had twenty minutes. That should be enough time to get stamps.

Mrs. Detwiler raised her voice. "Maybe *Mr.* Winslow is not busy."

"He's putting up prescriptions for Doctor Fagan, but Josie can help you."

Wait on Mrs. Detwiler? I'd rather have measles.

Billy poked through our display of school supplies. "I don't want to go to New Brunswick," he said. "Besides, they have paper and pencils here."

Mrs. Detwiler glared at her son. "You need a *nice* fountain pen and ink," she said. "We are going to New Brunswick, and that's final."

"Buy me some licorice."

Not even "please," I thought as I went to get the stamp drawer key from Dad. Boy am I glad he does not go to my school. We'd be in the same grade.

"Tiny, go see the baby," I coaxed. Tiny was not allowed behind the register when we were doing business. "Maybe you can help her stop crying."

"Can I have my candy first?"

Billy mocked my sister. "Can I have my candy first?"

"After you help the baby," I said to Tiny.

Mrs. Detwiler drummed her fingers on the counter as Tiny tried to open the candy case.

"No. Not now." I pushed the sliding door to the candy shut.

"Never mind your sister," Mrs. Detwiler ordered. "I need stamps, and that trolley will be here any minute." Mrs. Detwiler plopped her handbag on the counter.

"How many stamps would you like?" I asked, unlocking the stamp drawer under the cash register.

Mrs. Detwiler looked at the ceiling as she counted on her fingers.

With his mother occupied, Billy sneered at me. "Pharmacy Girl." It was no compliment.

I bit my lip. I couldn't be rude to customers — not even Billy. We'd lose business.

"Twenty," said Mrs. Detwiler, scowling at Mrs. Johnson's crying infant. "No, eighteen."

As I separated a row of first-class Washingtons along the perforations, Tiny climbed on a stool to watch me. "No, Tiny, you can't be here. Get down."

As I continued detaching stamps, Mrs. Detwiler snapped, "I didn't want first class. I asked you for postcard stamps."

What? She hadn't said anything about postcard stamps, had she?

Billy scoffed, "What do you expect from a girl? She can't even get the right stamps."

I wished I were a boy. I'd punch him right in the kisser.

Mrs. Detwiler rummaged through her purse, muttering, "Doesn't listen. Probably can't count. Slow as molasses." She pointed a finger at me. "If I miss that trolley, it will be your fault."

My cheeks burned. I switched to penny postcard stamps as fast as I could. "That will be eighteen cents, please."

Mrs. Detwiler pushed a dollar over the counter and recounted the stamps. "At least make sure you count the change correctly. You can do that much, *can't* you?"

I wanted to cry and shout all at the same time. *I can count change! I've been helping in the store for over a year, ever since my father opened for business when I was in the sixth grade. You never said you wanted postcard stamps! And your stupid trolley won't be here for —*

"What's this?" Tiny had reached in the stamp drawer.

I froze.

"Oh good God!" Mrs. Detwiler screeched. "The child has a gun!"

"DADDY!" I yelled. "Tiny has the revolver!"

Do something. Blood pounded in my ears. *Stop her.* I tried to grab Tiny's arm.

"STOP!" Dad was behind me. "Hold still!" He grabbed the gun barrel and moved it toward the wall away from all of us. "Clementine, I'm going to take the gun out of your hand. Don't do anything until I say so. Do you understand?"

Dad guided the gun out of Tiny's hand and pointed it at the floor. "Clementine, wait outside the back door."

Tiny's eyes grew big and watery as a quivering frown covered the bottom of her face. I lifted her off the stool. Suddenly, I felt sorry for my sister.

Mother helped Mrs. Johnson and the baby up from the floor where they had taken cover behind the soda fountain. The baby screamed even more. Mrs. Detwiler and Billy stood petrified in front of the post office counter. Billy's eyes popped out of their sockets.

Still pointing the gun at the floor, Dad opened the gun and rotated the part where the bullets were. He said, "Everything's under control now. Ladies, I am so very sorry."

"Under control? Under control?" Veins stood out on Mrs. Detwiler's neck. "She could have killed me!"

Still pointing the gun away from everyone, Dad rechecked the weapon. I knew he was rotating the cylinder so the first two chambers would be empty. Then he locked the gun back in the drawer.

"I *am* sorry, Mrs. Detwiler. Tiny is not supposed to be behind the register when we are doing business. Believe me, I'm going to have a serious discussion with her as soon as we've taken care of you and Mrs. Johnson."

Mrs. Detwiler bristled. "A lot of good that does!"

Handing Mrs. Detwiler her dollar, Dad said softly, "Mrs. Detwiler, would you like a drink of water?"

"Yes, Gretchen," Mother said. "Maybe you should sit down."

"Humph!" She took her stamps and her dollar. As she and Billy left the store, Billy kept looking back at the post office counter. Mrs. Detwiler slammed the screen door open so hard the shop bell only jangled once before it stuck. She yanked her son outside by his shirtsleeve. I thought the screen door had come off its hinges, but it slowly swung back and banged several times before it finally closed.

Mrs. Johnson, looking a little pale, shushed her baby. Mother scowled. I couldn't tell if she was madder at Tiny, Mrs. Detwiler, or me.

Dad pulled change out of his pocket and handed me the stamp drawer key. I put the money in the drawer and gave the key back. I'd never seen him look so strange. He was gray. "Phew, *I* could use a drink." Dad mopped his brow with his handkerchief. "I need something cold."

Dad went behind the soda fountain and pumped Coca-Cola syrup into a short glass. "Mrs. Johnson?" She

8

nodded. He held up an empty glass. "Ethel?" He poured syrup and seltzer from the fountain into two more glasses.

I was not allowed to have soda. Dad asked if I wanted lemonade. I shook my head no. Right now, I didn't think I could even manage a Mary Jane.

My sister stood outside the screen door whimpering. "Daddddyyy, I want a drink." Tiny leaned her head and arms on the middle crosspiece on the door. Her face pressing against the screen, she lightly kicked the wood at the bottom. "Pleeeeze. I'm sorrry," she whined.

Mother asked Dad if he wanted her to deal with Tiny. She meant a spanking. Dad put his glass down and said, "I better do this now so Tiny understands what she did wrong."

Mrs. Johnson said she needed to get home. Mother apologized again for Tiny and the gun as she walked Mrs. Johnson to the front door.

As I washed the used glasses, I heard Dad and Tiny outside. He did not yell, but he sounded stern enough to make my stomach knot.

"You cannot touch the gun. This is serious, Clementine. This is the most important thing I will tell you in your whole life. Never touch the gun."

Tiny sobbed. "Yes, Daddy."

"Let this be a lesson to you. No guns."

9

In between sobs she asked, "Are you going to spank me?"

"Daddy, don't!" I ran to the back door, hands still dripping from rinsing glasses. "Don't spank her! It's my fault," I stammered. "Daddy, I'm so sorry. I should have stopped her!"

"It's all right, Josie. I saw what was going on. You tried, Mrs. Detwiler was being difficult, and Tiny didn't listen. And I'm not going to spank her."

No? I was surprised.

"This is too important for just a spanking." He turned to my sister. "Clementine, you are *banished* from the store for a month. That means you cannot come in the store for any reason. *And* there will be no ice cream, and there will be no candy, starting now."

He turned to me. I hoped and prayed I wouldn't be banished too. "Josie, you'll need to stay with Tiny until Grandma comes home. And give her a drink. It's awfully hot out here."

I never thought there could be something worse than a spanking. Banishment sounded so — so lonely. At least no one was hurt. But if Tiny couldn't go in the store, someone would have to watch her. Right now that someone was me. Would Gram be back in time for me to go to the library? Could I tell Grace about the gun? Would my parents let us go to tomorrow's picnic? And what about Labor Day? Would I have to watch Tiny instead of going to the parade? My head hurt. Oh Tiny, why did you pull the gun from the drawer!

CHAPTER TWO

THE PICNIC ON THE RARITAN

Late in the afternoon of the next day, we walked with our families down to the river for an early Labor Day picnic.

"I took your book back to the library and got you number three, *Snow Camp,*" Grace said. "It's at my house."

"Thanks. I don't know what I'd do if I had to wait a week to read the next Ruth Fielding."

Grace and I trailed behind everyone as we pulled Tiny and baskets of food in a little wagon.

"Did your parents let you go alone to New Brunswick?"

"No, they made George go with me since you couldn't go to the library."

She stopped walking and stared at me. "I still can't believe your sister pulled the gun out in front of Mrs. Detwiler. Of all people!"

I nodded.

"I don't envy you. That Mrs. Detwiler is a blabberer. I bet she's told everyone in town," Grace said.

I shuddered. "It's so embarrassing."

"Hey, you slowpokes!" Grace's brother, Frank, ran up to hurry us along. "Up and at 'em, girls. You don't want to miss out on all the eats!"

"I think *you* don't want to miss out on all the eats," Grace sassed.

Mother had spread an old quilt on the ground, and Grace's mother, Mary, was setting out platters of fried chicken and potato salad.

"Josie, watch your sister, please. Don't let her get in the water," Mother said. "Tiny, keep your shoes on and stay out of the river."

Grace and I followed Tiny down to the water. Other picnickers dotted the riverbank. The sun was low on the New Brunswick side, its rays sending a thousand glints of light rippling off the water.

"What's the fun in having a picnic by the river if you can't go in?" Grace asked.

"Or if you have to watch your sister like a hawk?" I responded, knowing full well that Tiny would be tempted to ignore Mother's instructions.

"Don't look now." Grace pointed at my sister.

Tiny was sitting in the wet sand pulling off her socks.

"Good night! How can she get her shoes off so fast?"

Grace helped me brush the sand off her feet and put her socks and shoes back on.

Tiny pouted.

"Who wants a hot dog?" I asked, trying to distract her as I cleaned dirt off her fingers with the hem of my dress. "Look. Frank and George have already made a little fire, so we can roast the frankfurters on a stick. Let's go see."

Back at our picnic spot, Mother and Gram had unpacked sliced tomatoes, cucumbers, and jars of lemonade. Frank and George were already into their mother's fried chicken.

"You leave some of that chicken for the rest of us," Mrs. Gardener scolded.

Still chewing a drumstick, Frank sat down with Tiny and showed her how to hold a hot dog on a stick near the flames. George finished a chicken wing and pulled another one from his pocket.

"I wish we knew who our teacher will be," I said as I kept a close eye on Tiny.

"Better hope you don't get old Miss Morrison," Frank warned. "She's been teaching eighth grade for the past hundred years."

"Boy, is she strict. No foolishness in her class," George said. "She rapped Frank's knuckles with a ruler for talking."

"Oh! Listen to you!" Frank exclaimed. "I never got detentions nor had *my* ears pulled!"

We laughed. George threw a chicken bone at his brother. Frank handed me Tiny's hot dog stick and scrambled to his feet. George knew he was in trouble and took off.

"I bet they end up soaking wet," Grace said as we watched the boys scamper away.

We went back to talking about school and what we'd wear the first day. Grace said, "My mother finished my dress. It's got a dropped waist and a sailor's collar, like the one we saw in *McCall's.* Are you wearing the new middy blouse?"

I had saved money from my paper route and splurged on a new blouse from Young's Department Store. As I helped turn Tiny's hot dog over, I said, "You don't think it's too fancy, do you? You know, with the tucks and the lace?"

"It's absolutely cunning!" Grace cried. "We're going to look splendid!"

Suddenly I felt water dripping on my back. Frank and George stood directly behind us, shaking water from their hands and arms on Grace and me.

Grace jumped up. "Get away from us! You're sopping wet!"

The boys looked like two drowned rats.

"Oh no! You're drenched!" Mrs. Gardener shooed her sons away. "You two go straight home and take baths. Who knows what's in that river water. You could get polio. And put those wet clothes right in the laundry tub."

"Save us some dessert!" George shouted as they ran off.

"Wish we had been able to go swimming," I said to Grace.

"They have all the fun," she said, scowling.

The boys were back in time for dessert.

"Did you take a bath?" Mrs. Gardener asked her sons.

They nodded, but I had a feeling their slicked back hair was still wet from river water.

Gram cut pieces of peach cake, and Dad scooped ice cream onto our plates. When Tiny came to get ice cream, he shook his head. Before Tiny could put up a fuss, Dad shushed her. "Do you remember yesterday? Tell me why you cannot have ice cream."

My sister looked at the ground. "I touched the gun," she said in a small voice.

"You may have cake—but no ice cream." Dad handed her the plate.

But Tiny let the plate tilt, and the cake slid onto the ground. Dropping the plate, she ran to Mother and hid her face in Mother's skirt.

"Doctor Fagan was in the store yesterday," Mother told Mrs. Gardener, ignoring Tiny so she would not wind herself up into a crying fit. "He told Joe about influenza coming into New York City on ships from Europe."

"It's too early for flu," Gram said. "Old people and babies have to be careful about flu because it can turn into pneumonia."

Grace's mother asked, "Joe, what about this flu in New York City?"

Dad wiped his face with his napkin. "Two weeks ago, there was a Norwegian ship in New York that sent ten people to the hospital with what might have been Spanish influenza. Nearly two hundred people were sick during the crossing. Mostly third-class passengers. Four died, including one of the ship's cooks, but authorities didn't think well-fed passengers were affected."

"Don't worry, Mom," Frank chirped. "Look at George. He's the picture of well fed."

We laughed.

"Still, flu is contagious," Mother said. "Two hundred people onboard getting sick like that. Luckily, flu is not usually life threatening like typhoid."

"Or cholera," said Mrs. Gardener.

"Or diphtheria," added Gram. "Measles, for that matter."

"Polio," I said. Polio scared me. You could be paralyzed or even die.

Dad swallowed more cake. "Health authorities are treating the patients for pneumonia."

Poking her fork in the air to make a point, Grandma said, "Pneumonia is the old man's friend. You are not sick for very long, there's not much pain, and you just drift off as if to sleep. Except you wake up in heaven."

"But that's the thing, Mother," Dad said. "A second ship had four crew members die along with a twenty-one-year old passenger. You would think crew members would be young and healthy. You would think they could fight off the disease and any subsequent pneumonia." Dad finished his cake and ice cream. "We don't know the whole story. We'll have to wait and see."

"Now *you* sound like a doctor," Mother teased. "And it's getting dark. Maybe it's time to pack up."

We put the leftovers and dishes back into the picnic baskets.

While Frank and George put out the fire, my father asked them, "Would you like to make some extra money?"

"Sure, Mr. Winslow. What do you need done?" Frank asked.

"I need a hole dug in the backyard by the garage."

"What are you up to now?" Mother asked.

"I'm planting a spruce tree. And when the war's over, I'm decorating it with electric Christmas lights."

Christmas lights? We had electric Christmas lights on our tree in the house, but outside? Ever since Dad had seen the lighted outdoor tree in New York City at Madison Square, he was crazy to set up a tree of his own.

"How are you going to do that?" Mother asked.

"Haven't figured it out yet," Dad laughed.

"Let's get through Labor Day first," Gram said. "Big parade tomorrow."

Grace grinned and whispered, "Looks like you can go. What time do you want me to come over to decorate the wagon?"

"Ten o'clock."

It was dark when we walked home from the picnic. Dad carried Tiny, who was sound asleep. When we got to the alley that led to the back of our store, a kid on a bicycle came storming past and nearly ran us over.

"Well, that gave me quite a start." Gram held her hand over her heart, clearly rattled. "Who *was* that boy?"

Down the street there was a flash and a bang of a firecracker, then a boy's voice yelled, "Pharmacy Girl!"

I knew that voice. My skin crawled. "Billy Detwiler," I said.

As we approached the back of the store, we could see the screen door was stuck open.

"I thought I closed the screen." Dad checked the inside door. "This one's locked." He glanced at the bell as he wiggled the screen. It jingled, and the door closed on its own.

"What is Billy Detwiler doing coming out of the alley at this time of night?" Mother wanted to know. "And why is he yelling 'Pharmacy Girl'?" She looked at me.

I knew why. It was because Billy Detwiler hated me.

When Mother came in my room to say good night, I told her how Billy had called me "Pharmacy Girl" yesterday. Normally, my nickname made me feel grown up and responsible. But when Billy said it, I knew it was no compliment. "I don't know what I did to deserve him being so mean," I said. "That was before the, you know, the gun mess."

Mother smoothed my hair and the pillow. "Well, I am very proud of my pharmacy girl, so don't you worry about Billy Detwiler. Think about tomorrow and the parade."

"Can Tiny still come with us?"

"Yes, Tiny can come with you — as long as you use the wagon. She'll never be able to walk all that way. And

Grace is going to help you? Are you sure you want the responsibility?"

"Yes. Grace and I have planned to be in the parade ever since the Fourth of July. I can't desert her now."

Mother gave me a kiss on the forehead. "Good night, my pharmacy girl."

CHAPTER THREE

THE LABOR DAY PARADE

"Ouch! You stuck me!"

"I'm sorry. Hold still so I can pin this costume on you," I told Tiny. "You want to look like the Statue of Liberty in the Labor Day parade, don't you?"

Tiny frowned but held still.

Grace stopped decorating the wagon. "I'm surprised your parents let Tiny be in the parade. I mean, after Saturday."

"She can't go in the store, Dad's at the parade, and Mother and Gram will be busy with customers before and after the parade. So I'm stuck with Tiny." I hoped Grace didn't mind a tag-a-long sister today. "Besides, I think I'd die if we couldn't be in the parade. We've been planning all summer, and we bought all this crepe paper." I looked at the yards of red, white, and blue draped on the wagon and felt a twinge of regret. I was the one who was supposed to keep Tiny out of trouble.

Grace pulled the wagon around so we could see the other side. "Are we patriotic enough?"

We draped another layer of red, white, and blue streamers around the wagon just in case.

"Now for Tiny's crown of sunbeams." I put the cardboard headpiece on my sister. It was too big and slipped over her eyes.

"I have extra hair pins," Grace said.

I straightened the sunbeams and fastened the headpiece so Tiny could see. "Try to hold still," I said, but I didn't think it would stay on more than five minutes.

Since it was still summer, we wore white dresses. We pinned red and blue ribbons across our shoulders like sashes and made red and blue bows for our hair. Dressed and ready, we were off, our miniature Statue of Liberty in tow, heading down Raritan Avenue toward the staging area by the bridge.

We found Dad with the volunteer firemen. He looked handsome and brave in his dark-blue dress uniform. Earlier, Mother had said he looked "dashing," and Dad joked that all firemen were dashing. "Who wants a fireman who *walks* to a fire?" he asked. Mother shooed him out the door.

Dad let us climb on the fire engine for a better view. Since America had joined the Great War, troops regularly marched through town. I would hear them at night marching up Raritan Avenue to Hoboken to board troop ships headed for France.

"Holy smokes," said Grace, her eyes wide with astonishment. "There must be a thousand soldiers. They're all the way across the bridge and up Albany Street."

"Shush." Dad put his finger to his lips, but I could see he had a twinkle in his eye. "There might be spies around. We don't want the Germans to know our troop strengths."

"Daddy." I gave him a pretend serious look. "Couldn't a spy just stand here and count them?"

In front of us, officers' horses nickered and tossed their heads. Dad smiled and checked his pocket watch. "Won't be long now. The fire bell will signal the start of the parade at noon. There'll be a warning bell five minutes before."

We watched more people arriving—mostly kids on scooters and decorated bicycles. Billy pedaled by the fire truck. "Hey, Pharmacy Girl! Is your little sister gonna' shoot anybody today?"

Everybody could hear him. What would people think? I wanted to hide.

"Don't take the bait," Dad warned. "We've got a little time. Let's meet some soldiers." Dad helped Tiny off the fire engine.

"That Billy Detwiler!" I sputtered to Grace as we climbed down.

"At least we don't have to put up with him in school."

"Thank goodness he goes to Rutgers Prep."

We followed Dad as he walked from soldier to soldier, shaking hands, making conversation, wishing the young men good luck.

Grace whispered, "My brother could be one of them. Now that the draft age has been lowered, if the war doesn't end by Memorial Day, Frank will be eighteen, graduated, and have to go into the army."

I could tell Grace was worried. I didn't mention that the draft age had been raised as well and our fathers were now eligible too. I couldn't think about that.

"Frank's brave. He'll probably volunteer," I said. I liked Frank. He wasn't one of those brothers who had no use for little sisters or their friends. I linked arms with Grace. "Let's hope the war will be over by then."

It was almost time for the parade to start. The Boy Scout color guard, their flags hanging motionless in the heat, took its place in front of the Rutgers band. A Packard with an open top pulled in behind the musicians. The mayor and two elderly Civil War veterans got in the car. Younger veterans, dressed in their Spanish-American War uniforms, joined ranks with the soldiers who were young enough to be their sons.

Suddenly there was a loud bang. Everyone jumped. It was only a firecracker, but still, soldiers flinched and horses whinnied.

"Whoa, Neddy!" We turned to see Mr. Gephardt having trouble keeping Old Ned steady. Ned was the town's fire horse, and he was big and strong, part speedster and part draft horse. Now that the firemen had the new La France fire engine, they didn't need Ned anymore. But for old time's sake, Ned still pulled the hose cart in parades.

Mr. Gephardt had just settled Ned when the bell on the firehouse started clanging. Ned reared and took off, hauling the hose cart and Mr. Gephardt with him. People scattered. Mr. Gephardt pulled on the reins with all his might while men sprinted after the runaway horse. Dad took off for the hose cart and grabbed for the back handlebars, but he caught the bars too low. He couldn't get his footing on the running board, and the runaway horse and hose cart dragged Dad up the street.

"Daddy!" I screamed.

Ned barreled up Raritan Avenue where spectators waited to see the parade. Halfway up the hill, Dad let go and lay in the street.

"Josie! Look out!" It was Grace. I turned. Two soldiers on horseback came at a full gallop. I pulled Tiny away.

Up the street, Dad covered his head with his arms and rolled into a ball. One horse veered clear of Dad. The other jumped over him. I ran to help my father. Onlookers helped Dad up, and together we made it back to the fire engine.

We sat on the fire truck's running board. Tiny wanted to sit on Dad's lap, but I made her sit between Grace and me. Dad's trousers were torn, and there was blood and dirt on his knees.

"Holy smokes! I thought for sure we were going to get trampled," Grace whispered.

"Me too."

We looked up Raritan Avenue, but couldn't see over the rise in the road. "I hope no one was hurt," I said.

An officer came over to us. "I'm Walter Parsons, Company Surgeon."

"Joe Winslow." They shook hands. "Pharmacist, volunteer fireman, and town idiot."

"Pretty heroic," the doctor said.

"Pretty stupid in hindsight," Dad groused.

The doctor took supplies out of his leather bag. I helped roll up Dad's pant legs, and the doctor gently felt around Dad's knees. "No fracture that I can tell." He poured antiseptic onto gauze. "This is going to sting," he warned as he started cleaning Dad's knee.

"I know." Dad winced.

As the doctor worked, my dad asked questions. "What do you know about influenza coming from Europe?"

"We've heard conflicting reports of flu from the trenches all summer. The Navy said Spanish influenza was rampant in Switzerland. The Brits say it's over. Other reports say French soldiers are so sick with three-day fever they've been hospitalized, and a fair number are dying from subsequent pneumonias. Even the Germans have Spanish influenza."

Suddenly, a hush came over the crowd.

"It's the two soldiers on horseback," Grace said, craning her neck to get a better view. "But I don't see Ned or Mr. Gephardt."

"Where's the hose cart?" I hoped they didn't have a wreck.

"They're waving," Grace said. "Maybe that means everything is okay."

The soldiers rode straight toward the La France and dismounted. One soldier spoke with the commanding officer and the fire chief. The other came over to see us, and he apologized for nearly running us down. "That old fire horse is a humdinger. He nearly took us clear out of town before we could slow him down. But Old Neddy's safe and sound back at the firehouse with Mr. Gephardt."

29

The surgeon finished bandaging Dad's knees. Chief McMurtry got up on the La France and announced that Ned and Mr. Gephardt were too tuckered out to do any more today and that they were both having a glass of beer at the firehouse.

The crowd laughed.

Someone shouted, "Hey, McMurtry! There are children here!"

The chief held up his hands. "It's all right, kids. Ned's of age and Gephardt has permission from his wife."

More laughter.

"Seriously, thanks to these two brave soldiers who ran down Old Ned," he said, pointing to the heroes, "nobody was hurt! Well, except Joe Winslow, but he looks like he's going to be okay."

The crowd applauded.

The chief clapped his hands together. "We've got to start this parade right away. These brave soldiers have to get to France!" He shot his fist up in the air. "General Pershing's orders!"

Grace and I cheered with everyone else.

The Boy Scouts got back in place, and the Packard started right up. Officers sent the call to march echoing down the line of waiting soldiers. The drum major's baton sparkled in the sun. He blew his whistle, and with one breath, the band struck up "The Stars and Stripes Forever."

As the Boy Scouts reached the top of the hill, a light breeze caught the American flag and gently unfurled the heavy silk. Grace and I sang along: "Three cheers for the red, white, and blue—" Suddenly my nose tickled inside, and I felt goosebumps on my arms as if I had a chill. I was crying. I had no idea why.

Tiny climbed in the wagon, and I straightened her sunbeams. "Is it time to wave?"

"It sure is!"

As the soldiers marched past, we waved until we thought our arms would fall off. Here and there, soldiers smiled and winked or waved back at us. Then we joined bikes, scooters, and wagons like ours and marched up Raritan Avenue. The La France was last, the truck's fire bell clanging out an ear-splitting racket.

When we were in front of our store, Gram gave us a drink, and Mother fumbled with the Kodak. "That's it. Hold still now."

Firecrackers went off nearby.

"Fiddlesticks," Mother said. "I think I moved."

"Hold your breath when you push the lever down," I said, remembering what Dad had taught me.

She advanced the film. "Smile," Mother sang. *Click.* The shutter engaged. "Got it. Now off with you. Finish the parade."

31

～

Afterwards, we found Mr. Gephardt and Doctor Fagan in the store ribbing Dad about chasing the old hose cart. Dad was in the wood-and-cane wheelchair we had for customers, and he had ice bags perched on both of his knees. Even though the men were laughing, Mother and Gram fussed over him.

"What is Tiny doing in here?" Grandma asked, and everyone stopped to look at us.

Tiny danced around. "I have to pee," she said, running for the back of the store.

"Let her use the bathroom." Mother waved us to go catch up with Tiny.

As Grace and I waited for my sister, I noticed the screen door at the back of the store was wide open. Again. But when I tugged the door to close it, the bell hanging on the frame did not jingle. Now, that *was* unusual. When I looked up, there was paper wadded inside the bell.

"Holy smokes." Grace pointed to a neat slit near the hook-and-eye lock. "The screen is ripped."

I looked. "Or cut." I stepped around to the front of the store. "Mother, there's something wrong with the—" As I came to the post office counter, I stopped. The stamp drawer hung open.

"Josie, how many times do we have to remind you not to raise your voice in the store?"

I pointed at the drawer.

32

"What's this?" Mother exclaimed.

Dad got out of the wheelchair, ice bags falling on the floor. Everyone came to look.

"Damn!" he cursed.

Dad never swore!

"Let's see what's missing," he said, hobbling behind the counter.

Nothing appeared to be gone. The gun was under the stamps and the ledger. Dad carefully picked up the revolver and checked the chambers the way he had Saturday. I looked for Tiny. She was still in the bathroom.

The men inspected the damaged drawer.

"Jimmied," said Mr. Gephardt, running his finger across the splintered wood and mangled lock.

I picked up a screwdriver from the floor. "Is this ours?"

"I think we have the weapon," Dad said as he examined the screwdriver and held it near the gouges on the drawer. "Josie, what did you want to tell your mother?"

I showed everyone the slit in the screen and the paper in the shop bell.

Doc Fagan pulled the paper out. "Fireworks wrapper."

"Whoever did this knew about the door and the bell," Dad said. "And knew we'd be out too."

33

"That could be anybody in town," Doctor Fagan said.

While Gram and Mother recounted everything they could remember about the afternoon, I poured lemonade for Grace and my sister.

Mother remembered taking our picture and giving us a drink. "Wasn't that when we heard the firecrackers in the alley?"

Grace and I checked outside and found spent firecrackers and scorch marks on the ground. The fireworks wrapper was the same kind we had found muffling the shop bell. We gave the evidence to Dad.

"Thank you, girls. Josie, please take Tiny outside," Dad said.

Cat's whiskers! The banishment was still in force. "I wish I could hear what they were saying in the store," I said once we were outside.

"Me too," said Grace.

Finishing our drinks on the back steps, Grace whispered, "I can't believe someone tried to rob your store." She tilted her head back and tapped the bottom of her glass to get the last of the lemonade. "Your dad's really mad," she said, chomping a mouth full of ice. "If it had been my father, he would have said more than," she dropped her voice, "d-a-m-n."

"Has anyone ever tried to rob your dad's butcher shop?" I asked.

She shook her head. "No."

"Us either."

"Who would do such a thing?" Grace asked.

I sipped my lemonade. "Someone with firecrackers."

"What grown-up would use firecrackers?"

"Not a grown-up." Lemonade and ice burned and froze my stomach all at the same time. "A kid. A kid would use firecrackers."

CHAPTER FOUR

SCHOOL BELLS RING

The first day of school was the day after Labor Day. After dismissal, I couldn't wait to tell my parents the good news. I ran into the store, letting the screen door bang. "Mother, Dad, you'll never guess who my teacher is!" I twirled across the store to the soda fountain.

"Let's see." Dad said. "President Wilson?"

"No," I giggled.

"Thomas Edison?"

I rolled my eyes.

Prolonging the drama, Dad looked up to heaven and asked, "Mrs. Detwiler?"

"No! Daddy, be serious. It's Miss Penny! She moved up a grade with us!"

My parents had sneaky little smiles on their faces.

"You knew! You knew all along, didn't you?"

They confessed. Dad was on the school board, and although he knew a lot about the school, he never talked about it with me.

Behind the soda fountain, I dished up a scoop of peach ice cream. In between bites I told Mother and Dad about school. "Everybody was really happy to have MP— I mean, Miss Penny again." Last year, Grace and I had nicknamed our teacher MP. "Grace and I are sitting together. It was funny. We all took our old seats. It made Miss Penny laugh, so she let us stay in those seats." I crunched down on a piece of frozen peach. "'e're 'oing to do all sorts of projects for 'ivics—learning about our country and our government and what it means to be patriotic. Similar to 'ast 'ear." I ate another spoonful.

"Josie, try not to speak with your mouth full," reminded my mother.

I swallowed. "I'm not sure if we'll be knitting again. Miss Penny said the Red Cross has enough afghans." I took the last bite of ice cream and let it melt in my mouth. "We're going to raise money for the next Liberty Loan Drive. Miss Penny wants us all to make Four-Minute Speeches like the ones we heard at the theater, and we're going to have a class election."

"Sounds like you had a good day," Mother said.

I licked the spoon and put my dish in the sink. "Well, except for Billy Detwiler. It turns out he's in our class! Why isn't he at Rutgers Prep this year?"

Neither of my parents said anything.

"Did you know Billy Detwiler's given name is Wilhelm, not William? When Miss Penny was taking roll she called him 'Wilhelm,' and he got smart with her." I waited for the tap water to get hot so I could wash the dish and the spoon. "He was *rude* to Miss Penny. Billy said his mother had made it clear to the principal that he was not to be called Wilhelm."

"I bet she made it clear," my mother grumbled. "What did Miss Penny do?"

"She just said, 'All right, Billy,' and wrote something in the roll book. But I could see her neck getting red. I think she was annoyed with him. I know I would be. But Miss Penny never yells. Anyway, when Billy came back to school from lunch, his mother came with him. She marched right into school. Billy told us kids that his mother was going to tell Miss Penny a thing or two."

As I put the dish and the spoon on the drain board, I thought it was unfair that Billy got Miss Penny in trouble for calling him Wilhelm. I wondered if he was mean enough to try to rob our store.

"What's so bad about Wilhelm?" I asked. "Why would Mrs. Detwiler not want anyone to call him Wilhelm? I mean, that's what she named him."

"Times change," said Mother. "When he was a baby it didn't matter. Now it's different. You know Wilhelm is the German Chancellor's name."

Oh, Kaiser Wilhelm. Ha! I laughed to myself. *Kaiser Billy. It suits the old meanie.*

Mother continued, "You know how people are about anything German." Then she changed the subject. "What else happened at school?"

"We're going to have an arithmetic test tomorrow. Miss Penny wants to see how much we remembered over the summer. She's giving us the same test we took last June. I got one hundred percent last time, so it should be easy." I climbed up on a stool by the counter. "Grace thinks I should run for class president."

"What do *you* think?" asked Dad.

"I don't like making speeches in front of everybody. Besides, Billy told everyone at recess he was running for class president and he dared anyone to run against him."

"You should run," Mother said.

A loud thud at the front door let me know that the deliveryman had left the bundle of newspapers for me to deliver.

Out front, I read the headlines as I folded papers to fit in my news bag. "Allied victories at Drocourt-St. Quentin." "Americans bomb Hun Depots." Miss Penny will ask us where Drocourt-St. Quentin is. I knew it was somewhere in France. Maybe the war will end soon now that the Allies are getting closer to Germany. The paper makes things sound like everything is going our way. But another headline made my stomach ache. "Plan Registration of 18- to 45-Year-Old Men for Draft." If we are winning, why is there going to be another draft? Why do we need older men to go into the army now? Dad will have to register. What if he had to go to France? What if . . .

Tiny pulled my sleeve. "Can I go with you?"

"Did Mother say you could?"

She nodded yes.

"Can you bring the wagon around front?"

I wondered how far I would get delivering papers before she needed to ride.

∂

After dinner I did my homework at the kitchen table: a page of arithmetic, an essay about my favorite place, and a map to go with it.

Dad had his legs propped up on a chair with a pillow and ice bags on his knees. He read the paper and finished his coffee. Gram gave Tiny a bath, and Mother washed dishes.

I had just started some division when Dad flopped down the paper. "Can you believe they are talking about Christmas already! It says people should shop early for Christmas. Says we can help Santa and not interfere with war production by shopping now and bringing our packages home instead of having them delivered. We just barely got past Labor Day, and now we're talking about Christmas!"

I heard little feet running in the hall and then Gram's voice. "Get back here! You're all wet."

"Is Santa coming?" Tiny stood dripping in the kitchen doorway. The towel wrapped around her was useless.

"Not yet," Dad said with a chuckle. "It's only September. We're just talking about how we might help him when the time comes."

"Tiny, get back in the bathroom. You've got water on the floor." Mother was none too pleased. She grabbed kitchen towels and wiped up the puddles. "Any more news about the flu in New York City?" she asked.

"Hmmmm, no, don't see anything. But the suffragists and the anti-suffrage girls are at it again in the letters to the editor. I have to say the women's vote crowd writes a better argument."

Dad was quiet for a while, and I did more arithmetic.

Finally, he turned and looked at Mother. "Looks like I'll be registering for the draft next week after all."

"Can't you be excused because you are a druggist?" I asked. "Don't people need medicine here?"

"Maybe. But if the army needs doctors and nurses, they probably want pharmacists too." He patted my hand. "Don't worry 'til the time comes."

Over Dad's shoulder, I could see my mother at the sink wiping her eyes with her shirtsleeve. I looked at my arithmetic. What was seven times eight? I couldn't remember. I wrote down forty-five.

CHAPTER FIVE

THE TROUBLE WITH BILLY

Outside school the next morning, Grace and I waited with our classmates for the bell.

"*Josie get your gun, get your gun, get your gun . . . Take it on the run, on the run, on the run. Let your sister pull a gun, scare the wits from everyone . . .* " Billy was singing "Over There," but he had changed the words.

Why is he singing about me?

Grace grimaced. "What's he doing in our class anyway? He's just awful. Do you think he got kicked out of prep school?"

"Hey, Pharmacy Girl! Your little sister shoot anyone yet today?" Billy hollered. Boys standing around him sniggered. Girls stared at me.

Not again. My cheeks burning, I remembered Dad's advice—don't take the bait. I rolled my eyes at Grace, and we walked away, trying to ignore Billy.

The principal rang the bell for school to start. As we filed inside, Billy whistled "Over There."

"We are all gratified that you are so patriotic," the principal said as Billy passed, "but you need to be quiet now."

"Yes, sir!" Billy saluted.

I wanted to gag.

After we said the Pledge of Allegiance and sang "America," Miss Penny announced we would take the arithmetic test and started passing out the papers.

I heard humming. It was Billy again. Miss Penny asked him to be quiet.

I sneaked a glance across my row, and sure enough, Billy was giving me a smug face. He made me so angry I could feel my back tingle. I clenched my pencil and wanted to scream.

MP said, "I hope you all find this easy. You may begin."

Why did I look at him? Forget that bully, I told myself. Concentrate on the test. Add, subtract, multiply, and divide fractions and decimals — four-digit multiplication — long division. *I know how to do all this.* I even remembered the word problems from last June.

After the test, Miss Penny asked us to write an essay about what we had done to help the war effort over the summer. I wrote about collecting peach pits for soldiers' gas masks.

Just before noon dismissal, Miss Penny handed back our arithmetic tests. She said she was pleased that we remembered so much from last year, but there was no grade on my paper, only a number of red check marks. *This can't be mine.* I looked at my name on the front page. Yes, it was my test. I leafed through the test a second time. On the last page, there was a note, "Josie, please see me before you go home for lunch."

After the class left, Grace waited for me in the hall, and Miss Penny sat down in the desk next to mine. She took the arithmetic test that was still on my desk and pointed to the errors. "Josie, what happened? These seem to be just careless mistakes. This is not like you. You're a good arithmetic student."

I didn't know what to say. I never had a bad grade before and was too embarrassed to answer. I felt my chin quiver.

"Want to try again?" my teacher asked.

I nodded.

"Tonight, fix the mistakes, and tomorrow I will give you another test. And," she paused, "I want you to talk to your parents about this."

When I left the classroom, Grace was not in the hall. She hadn't waited after all.

Disappointed and relieved all at the same time, I headed home for lunch. I was not ready to tell anyone about my failure in arithmetic. Luckily when I got home, my parents were busy in the store, and Gram was canning tomatoes. Tiny and I ate tomato sandwiches and sliced peaches. I loved tomato sandwiches, but today they had no appeal. Gram noticed.

"Do you feel all right?" she asked. "You were a little late getting home for lunch."

I fibbed, "I'm fine. It's just hot, you know."

"I'll say." She dried perspiration from her forehead with her apron. "Just try standing over a steaming kettle of tomatoes."

I got ready to go back to school and gave Gram a hug.

"What's that for?" She looked at me, puzzled.

"Nothing," I said. The truth was I felt guilty about fibbing.

That was the morning. After recess, I found Grace on the school playground. "Why didn't you wait?" I asked.

"Oh, that Miss Morrison chased me and Billy out. She wouldn't even let me stay outside. 'Get home or you'll be late for the afternoon.'" Grace mimicked Miss Morrison's high-pitched voice.

"What were you doing with Billy?"

"That's what I need to tell you," Grace whispered.

But we were interrupted.

"Hey, Pharmacy Girl!" Billy called across the playground. "Did you tell your parents about your arithmetic test?" He smirked. "I got every problem right. Did you?"

How does he know about my arithmetic test?

"Girls are so dumb," Billy teased. "You should've seen Pharmacy Girl over here trying to count stamps and make change."

Grace whispered, "He's full of beans. Don't listen to him."

One part of my brain said, *You know he's a bully. He's just trying to get a rise out of you. Ignore him. Then he'll stop.* Another part of my brain said, *But what if it's true?* I failed the arithmetic test this morning. I had to tell my parents. Now everyone knew. My throat ached and my nose burned. Don't cry. Don't cry, I kept telling myself.

"Teacher's pet. *Stupid* teacher's pet," Billy mocked. "I know who won't be making honor roll this term."

That did it. I ran into the school, tears streaming down my face. In the girls' room, I hid in a stall and leaned my head against the partition and cried.

The girls' room door opened. "She came in here." It was Grace and a grown-up.

There was a gentle knock on the stall door. "Josie? Are you all right?" asked Miss Penny.

I opened the door and just stood there trying to catch my breath between sobs.

Miss Penny said, "Wash your face with cold water. Josie, dear, the last thing you need is to let Billy know he made you cry." She handed me a handkerchief. "Keep it. I hear the class coming."

I had cried so hard my nose ran. How embarrassing. I did not want MP to think me a crybaby.

I looked in the mirror over the sink—puffy eyes and a red nose. As I splashed my face, I hoped the cold water would do its job.

Grace and I hurried into our classroom. I tried to smile for Miss Penny, and she gave me a wink of encouragement. Janet came by my desk and whispered, "Don't worry, Josie. We all know Billy's as mean as a hornet."

I felt better, but only fifteen minutes into the afternoon, school had turned into a nightmare.

I perked up when Miss Penny read to us from *The Wind in the Willows*. But even MP's clever reading aloud couldn't keep my mind on the story. Billy's taunting about the gun and the test kept coming back.

On the way home after school, Grace chattered about getting a copy of the book MP was reading. Then she went merrily on to how we could raise money for the upcoming Liberty Loan Drive. I was glum and didn't say much.

"Josie, don't let him bother you," Grace said.

"How did he know?" I asked.

"That's what I wanted to tell you. When I was waiting for you at lunch, Billy was hanging around pretending to get a drink. But he was eavesdropping. Then Miss Morrison made us both leave."

"You heard what MP said about my test?"

Grace nodded. "I didn't mean to eavesdrop. I mean, not like Billy. And then I couldn't stay to wait for you. Are you cross with me?"

I smiled at her. "No, you're my best friend."

Grace said, "If Billy or anyone was picking on me like that, I'd be flustered too."

"He really is picking on me, isn't he?"

"Yep."

"Why?"

Grace shrugged. "Jealousy? He's a toad?"

I laughed, imagining Billy as a toad.

"But what if it's true? What if I'm not smart enough for arithmetic?"

"You've been the head of our class forever. Everyone knows you are an A student. Remember when you showed me how to subtract with zeros in the — what's its name? — you know, the top part of a subtraction problem."

"Minuend." I wanted to believe Grace.

"Minuend. Right." Grace planted herself in front of me. "Listen, I think you should run for class president again. You were president last year and everybody likes you. Who wants bossy old Billy ordering us around? He acts like he's the Kaiser. Maybe we should call him Wilhelm."

"And make him pick on me more?" I looked at Grace as if she were crazy.

"There are more girls in the class than boys. If all the girls vote for you, you can win."

"I don't know," I said and started walking.

"I'll help you!" Grace was not giving up. "We can't let dumb ol' Billy Detwiler spoil the fun of school."

We stopped in front of my father's store. "Think about it," said Grace. "You can tell me yes tomorrow."

That evening after dinner I showed my arithmetic test to my parents. They were surprised, and so was I because they were not angry. I redid the problems on the test, and Dad helped me make up new problems to practice for tomorrow.

Later that night I couldn't sleep. The electric fan hummed back and forth as it swept air across my bed. I kicked off my blankets and flipped my pillow so it would be cooler. I could hear Tiny snoring gently. But I kept thinking about Billy and the test. Had Billy flummoxed me that much? Was he going to harass me all year? If the rest of the year was anything like today, school was going to be awful. If I ran for class president, would things get worse?

CHAPTER SIX

THE CAMPAIGN

What a relief! I got 100 percent on my retest.

Bigger relief! Billy was too busy arguing with the boys about the World Series to bother me. Thank goodness for baseball.

Grace had already talked to Winnie and Janet. At recess, Janet pleaded with me to run for class president. She said her brother thought if Billy were elected, we'd all be sorry.

Grace gave me the I-told-you-so look.

Then my friends all jabbered at once: "Do it! Do it! We'll all help you. Come on!"

After school, delivering newspapers brought good news. The headlines said the Germans were retreating. And Gram made my favorite dinner: mashed potatoes and meatloaf. Mr. Hoover and the Food Administration would be proud of our efforts to conserve food. Breakfast was oatmeal—no wheat or meat. For lunch I had a tomato sandwich—bread from wheat, but no meat. Tonight, it was all right to have meat. Gram and Mother had stopped serving bread with dinner months ago and had substituted oatmeal for the bread in the meatloaf.

"Looks like someone's appetite has returned," Gram said.

"I'm stuffed." Dad pushed his plate away.

"I didn't mean you." Gram pretended to swat him with her napkin.

Dad sipped his coffee and made a face. "I'll never get used to coffee without sugar or cream." He started reading the paper, and I started my homework.

"Influenza's still coming in on ships from Europe," he said. "This time, only twenty-five cases. Sixteen hospitalized. Two died."

"What do you think that means?" Mother asked.

Dad shrugged. "I don't know. Yet."

He looked at my sister. "Tiny, get your book."

Tiny ran out of the kitchen. That was my cue.

"My friends are pestering me to run for class president again," I announced as I put my school things on the kitchen table. "Grace thinks I can win because there are more girls than boys in the class."

"Do *you* think you can win?" Dad asked.

I felt doubtful. "It could be close. There are seventeen girls in our class and fifteen boys."

"Can you take a loss? How will you feel if Billy wins? Can you be a good loser?" Dad asked.

I put my books on the table. "I guess I would be disappointed if I lost, but I think I can be a good sport."

"That's important," Dad said as Tiny climbed on his lap. Dad read a chapter from *Raggedy Ann*. I still liked to hear him read aloud, but tonight I had bigger fish to fry, namely, deciding if I would run for class president.

আ

On the way to school, I told Grace I would run but that I was afraid Billy would do something to get back at me.

"He's already picking on you," Grace said. "What do you have to lose?"

"What boy picks on a girl?"

"'A dastardly coward' is what Frank and George call him. They say that you have to stand up to a bully make them stop."

"Easy for boys to say."

"You need some brothers."

I laughed.

Once we were at school, we saw Mrs. Detwiler leaving the building, and when we got to the classroom, Principal Springfield was talking to Miss Penny. Neither of them was smiling. As Grace and I got in our seats, I said, "I think MP's upset. Her neck is red."

Grace looked at MP. "Detwiler, I bet." During arithmetic, Miss Penny announced that anyone who wanted to get a better grade on the arithmetic test could re-take it on Monday.

Billy stood up and started taking bows. *Had Billy's mother complained?*

In civics we reported on articles we read in the paper each night. I told how the Germans were retreating and blowing up their own supplies so the Allies couldn't use them. Most of the boys reported that the Boston Red Sox won the first game of the World Series, one to zero. Billy's news was that German soldiers chained women to machine guns to fight. I was shocked that anyone would think to do that. Could it be true? Are the Huns that awful?

Miss Penny talked about the class election next week. Monday would be nominations. Speeches and the vote would be Wednesday.

&

On Saturday the girls came over to help me get ready for the election. We made signs, thought up a cheer, a song, and drafted my speech. There were loads of things we could do this year like knitting, raising money, and rolling bandages. After we did our bit for the war effort, we could have some fun too. We could organize a class picnic with entertainment. I thought I should emphasize that we would do what the class wanted. I figured Billy would just dictate what he wanted to do. After the meeting we went downstairs to have ice cream in the store.

While I sprinkled chocolate Jimmies on ice cream, Winnie asked, "Who are the girls in the class we can count on to vote for Josie?" She started making a list. "Hattie, Nell, and Ruth. Violet and Flossie."

Flossie. We all looked at each other. Flossie could be a problem.

Grace said what I was thinking. "She likes boys, and I bet she'll vote for Billy just because he's a boy."

"Violet's Flossie's best friend. If Flossie votes for Billy, Violet will too," Janet added. "But maybe some boys will vote for you, Josie. I think we can count on Fred. He pals around with Tony Santorini. Maybe he can get Tony to vote for you too. The only problem is Fred told me that Billy threatened the boys, telling them they'd be sorry if he loses."

"Isn't Fred afraid Billy will cause trouble for him?" I asked.

"Nah," said Janet. "Have you seen how much my brother grew over the summer? All Fred has to do is hold his hand on Billy's forehead and Billy won't be able to land a punch. Billy's arms are too short to reach Fred."

I wished I had grown more over the summer.

Winnie's List

Votes for Josie	*Boys for Josie*
Hattie	Fred
Nell	
Ruth	*Votes for Billy*
Josie	Billy
Grace	Eugene
Winnie	Theodore
Janet	Howard
Nora	Leo
Marjorie	James
Lillian	Bob
Juanita	Ralph
Dorothy	John
Rebecca	Jacob
Edith	Jimmy
	Frank
Maybe for Josie	Ben
Mabel	
Flossie	
Violet	
Tony	

If all the girls vote for Josie and all the boys vote for Billy, we win, 17 to 15.

If we get Tony and Fred's vote, <u>Josie should win 19 to 13</u>.

If Flossie and Violet vote for Billy along with Mabel, and Fred and Tony vote for Josie, the vote will be 16 to 16. A tie.

If Tony and Fred vote for Billy, and Flossie and Violet do too, the vote will be 15 to 16. Billy wins.

Cheer

Josie is the best

Billy is a pest.   (Can't use that! Although it's true!)

Sing to "Over There"

Vote for HER	Have a care
Vote for HER	Don't just stare
She's the girl with the smarts	She's the girl with the smarts
Vote for HER	Vote for HER
'Cause the class is working	She will lead us
The class is working	She'll always please us
To do good deeds	And she's always fair
And win the war	She's the right one
	Vote for Her!

CHAPTER SEVEN

THE ELECTION

At school on Monday we found out what had happened with MP last Friday. Billy bragged how his mother complained to Principal Springfield that Miss Penny gave "preferential treatment" to one student by allowing her to retake a test.

Was MP in trouble because of me? Was I getting preferential treatment? Is Miss Penny only nice to me because my father is on the school board? Maybe she doesn't really like me . . .

At recess my friends and I talked to every girl in the class and told them I was running for class president. They all said they would vote for me. Even Flossie said she couldn't stand Billy.

When it was time for nominations, my heart beat faster.

Miss Penny started, "Do we have any nominations for class president?" Immediately three boys raised their hands and nominated Billy.

Miss Penny asked if there were any more nominations. Grace nominated me, and Winnie seconded the motion.

What happened next was a surprise. I never thought Billy would pull a stunt like this. He had a hissy-fit right there in class. He jumped out of his seat. "Women can't be presidents!" he blurted. "Women can't even vote! Maybe the girls shouldn't vote! That would be more like real life!"

My friends all started talking at once. "NO! Girls have always voted in school!"

Miss Penny tried to settle the class. "Billy, maybe you didn't know, but girls participate in class elections here at Lafayette."

Billy fumed. He pointed at me. "Just wait," he said under his breath.

I pretended that I wasn't bothered by Billy and flicked my head back around. But inside I was worried. What would he do next?

After school I got my answer. Billy followed me out of our classroom.

"Listen, you little pharmacy runt. You made a big mistake."

I kept walking. Grace and Janet caught up with me.

He hollered louder so everyone could hear. "Kids voted for you last year because you're Miss Penny's pet. Things are going to be different this year. Everybody's voting for me because everyone knows girls can't be presidents of anything."

"Says you!" Janet answered back. "Anyone who votes for you is just doing it because they're scared you'll beat them up!"

Janet was brave to sass him. Maybe having a twin brother made Janet not afraid to yell at a boy. We kept walking.

"You wait!" Billy yelled. "I said there would be trouble if anyone ran against me! You'll see!"

The next day, Billy put Flossie's hair in an inkwell. Poor Flossie sat right in front of Billy. She had long blonde hair that she still wore in old-fashioned ringlets.

"It was an accident," Billy told MP. "Flossie put her head back, and when her curls fell into the inkwell, I tried to get her hair out so they wouldn't be covered in ink."

What a liar. Flossie was in tears. Grace and I knew better. Grace sat next to me and Billy's seat was two desks over. We saw the whole thing. Grace raised her hand. "Miss Penny, that's not —"

I yanked her sweater and shook my head. "Later," I whispered. After the class left for lunch recess, we told Miss Penny what we had seen. I worried what Billy would do if he knew we had tattled. When we came back from lunch, Flossie's hair was damp and noticeably shorter. Ink stains and curls were gone. And so was Billy.

છે

On election day Grace said, "Hattie's absent. We need every vote now."

Miss Penny scheduled the speeches before lunch. When it was time, Billy said, "Ladies first."

Grace scowled. "What's he up to?"

I gave my speech the way we planned. I kept the new part about the four heroic women workers who died at the munitions plant explosion in Pompton Lakes. When I was done, there was applause. As I looked around the room, I noticed neither Violet nor Flossie was clapping. Flossie stared at the floor and played with what was left of her hair.

As I took my seat, Billy got up. The boys burst into cheers and applause. Why didn't we think to do that? Violet and Flossie clapped too. Billy held up his hands for quiet.

"Thank you for that resounding reception. If we were having a voice vote, I'd say I just won!"

More applause and whistles from the boys.

"As you know, I do not believe girls should vote or run for office, but I will abide by our school's traditions and congratulate Josie on a nice speech. Well, I think it was nice — I couldn't hear very much of it because of her itty-bitty girl's voice."

A few boys laughed. Miss Penny interrupted, "Billy, personal comments are inappropriate."

Billy continued. "I think certain jobs are for men, like being presidents of clubs and bosses at work. Did you know that my opponent has a paper route, which is a boy's job? She is stealing a job that really belongs to one of us."

Stealing a paper route from a boy? What a lot of bunk!

"And I believe men should work and women should stay home and tend to their knitting. General Pershing agrees with me. He ordered women not to go to France."

I wanted to jump out of my seat. *What? That's wrong! When did General Pershing say that?* What about all the nurses and canteen workers for the Red Cross? What about all the French-speaking American girls acting as operators on the telephone lines at the front that General Pershing requested? I thought I might explode.

Billy scoffed. "Black Jack Pershing is right. Staying home is for women. Knitting is for women. How many of you boys want to sit around knitting? There are other things boys can do for the war effort."

The boys cheered again.

"Yes, we had a girl class president last year, but we are older now and getting ready for high school. We need mature, male leadership. When one person gets special treatment, don't you wonder why? Could it be her father is on the school board? Could that be why she is a teacher's pet?"

Oh no! It sounded like something Billy's mother would say.

Miss Penny warned Billy again. "Any more personal remarks and I will have to ask you to stop your speech."

Billy continued, "I don't think my opponent is qualified for the job. She can't think on her feet in an emergency. You all know the gun story. Josie had no idea what to do. She just stared at her sister who was waving a loaded gun around and could have killed me. Her father had to take the gun away. Josie was useless."

"That's enough, Billy. Sit down."

Thank goodness Miss Penny was putting an end to Billy's lies.

Billy ignored Miss Penny. Talking fast, he said, "I also thought about those girls who got killed in the explosion. It proves girls cannot do dangerous work. That's not bravery. That's selfishness. That explosion could have killed hundreds of women at the plant—women with families to care for."

He was using my own argument about bravery against me.

Miss Penny stood at the front of the room. "Billy, you are done. Sit down. *Now.*"

As he went to his seat, Billy got in his parting shot. "In closing, I think you should vote for me and not for my opponent who is pampered and selfish."

The boys stood up and cheered. Two boys hoisted Billy up on their shoulders and marched him around the room as if he were a big hero. Miss Penny called for quiet and told them to put Billy down. As they started their second trip around the classroom, Miss Penny yelled, "That will do!"

We were stunned. Miss Penny *never* yelled. The boys nearly dropped Billy on the floor as they scurried back to their seats.

Grace slammed her fists down on her desk. "NO FAIR! Those are all lies!" She jumped up. "Josie is NOT SPOILED! The only spoiled brat around here is YOU, Billy Detwiler!"

Everyone talked at once. Miss Penny had to get out her whistle to get our attention. In a steely voice she said, "I think we will postpone the vote. Kindly take out your civics book and answer the questions on page twenty-eight." She wrote the page number on the board. "I think you need to review the differences between democracy and anarchy."

Billy started to protest, but Miss Penny simply turned around and glared at him. Her neck was the reddest I had ever seen.

We voted just before three o'clock. I lost by one vote. Even with Hattie absent, there were enough girls that I should have won. What happened?

Billy was yet again taking bows and boys were applauding. I looked at Grace. Her hand shot up. "Miss Penny, we demand a recount!"

Now the girls applauded. Boys booed. "There's no such thing!" Billy shouted.

"Actually, there is such a thing, and in close elections it is appropriate," Miss Penny said. "But the candidate has to ask for the recount. Josie? Do you want a recount?"

"Do it!" Grace said. "It's so close."

Winnie and Janet nodded their heads. Fred did too.

"Yes, Miss Penny. I'd like a recount."

Billy slammed his hands to his head and let out a loud "Arrgh!" Everyone had something to say.

"As soon as it is quiet," Miss Penny said.

The results were the same.

As we left school, Grace was still hot. "Unbelievable! I could just spit nails!"

Janet and Winnie put their arms around me and said how awful it was going to be to have Billy lording it over us all year. Violet flounced by with Flossie at her side. Not a word, but Flossie hung back a bit, and I wondered if she wanted to say something to me. Fred came by and playfully punched my arm. He didn't say a word about the election. Flossie walked on with Violet.

"Where did Billy get those votes?" Grace complained. "Fred?"

"I don't think so."

"Violet and Flossie? But they said they would vote for you!" Grace stopped and kicked some fallen leaves. "Flossie said she couldn't stand Billy. And after what he did to her hair . . . "

"Keep walking." I hooked my elbow into Grace's. "Let's not talk about it. It's over, and we're never going to know. It was a secret ballot." But I still wondered which of my friends had believed Billy's lies.

Grace walked with me all the way home. At the back door she said, "I'm sorry, Josie. I'm sorry I got you into this."

"Don't worry, Grace," I said. "I wanted to run."

When I got inside the store, I guess Mother and Dad could see my long face because they both stopped what they were doing. I sat on the little stool in the back of the pharmacy where customers could not see me. And then I cried. It was bad enough to lose to Billy, but it hurt even more to think my classmates believed all the bad things Billy had said about me. There was no holding back. The floodgates were open. I told my parents everything about Billy.

જ

When I woke up the next morning, I could hear birds chirping in the gutter above my window. And then I remembered. The election. And maybe not all my friends are really friends. Last night, Mother was upset by all the things Billy had been saying and doing. She wanted to know why I didn't tell her sooner. She also wanted to tell Mrs. Detwiler a thing or two, but Dad talked her out of it.

I sat on my bed in a fog. I felt like Ned, the fire horse, had dragged me down the street. Oh, how I wanted to stay home and not go to school!

Dad was gone by the time I got to breakfast. He wanted to register for the draft before the store got busy. Earlier this week the War Department said that men from thirty-one to thirty-six would be called up next. *Dad's thirty-five.* I wasn't in any mood to eat my oatmeal.

Gram said, "If you don't eat now, you will feel worse later. You need your energy today." She got up, and to my surprise, she got the sugar bowl out of the cupboard. She sprinkled real sugar on my oatmeal. "This is for medicinal purposes. You need strength to fight injustice."

I had to smile. "Gram, you're the best."

There was a knock on the back door. It was Grace. "I've come to escort you to school." She had a big smile on her face, and I knew she was trying to cheer me up.

Mother gave me a kiss on the forehead. "Be brave."

CHAPTER EIGHT

THE FIGHT

At school no one said anything to me about the election. It was like it never happened. I didn't know if I was disappointed that no one cared or if I was relieved. I wanted life to be normal and happy again.

All morning it was hard to concentrate on lessons because I couldn't help thinking about the election . . . and Dad. I was ashamed to think this—but I hoped he would not be called up to fight. I knew enough about the trenches and poisoned gas to know war was awful. Maybe the war would end before he had to go. I was being unpatriotic. I should be proud my dad might serve in the army.

After lunch I refilled my fountain pen. As I put the lid back on the inkwell in the desk, Billy picked up the pen, fiddling with the reservoir lever.

"Hey, Pharmacy Girl, what's this for?"

On the side of the pen is a lever that allows you to draw ink into a chamber. If you open the lever with ink in the pen, the ink comes back out.

Billy held the pen close to me. "Am I doing this right?" He pulled the lever out and ink squirted my middy blouse. He laughed.

"My blouse!" The words flew out of my mouth. "Ink's impossible to get out!"

"Josie! What's wrong?" Miss Penny exclaimed.

"Billy's ruined my middy!"

"It was an accident. I was just looking at her pen."

"That's not true! You did it on purpose!" I was still shouting.

"Liar," Billy answered.

"No, you're the liar," I snapped. "Just like when you lied about Flossie's hair."

"This squabbling needs to stop," Miss Penny warned.

Billy went for the last shot. "Your father's a slacker."

Without even thinking, I kicked Billy right in the shins as hard as I could.

While Billy hopped and howled, Fred egged me on. "Go ahead, Josie, let him have it!"

The class was in an uproar.

"My mother's going to hear about this!" Billy threatened.

"I'm sure of it," MP said through clenched teeth, and then in a voice I never dreamed she had, MP exclaimed, "ENOUGH!"

Miss Penny cast her eye around the room, and the noise stopped. "You know what to do if there is a fight." My classmates hurried into their seats.

Fight?

"Grace, ask Miss Morrison to come over, please."

Miss Morrison kept an eye on the class while MP escorted Billy and me to Mr. Springfield's office.

I'd never been sent to the principal before—not for being in trouble anyway. What would my parents say? I was in so much trouble. Oh, why did I kick him?

Billy limped and moaned all the way to the principal's office. "Why do *I* have to go to old Springfield? *She* kicked *me!*"

Inside the main office, Miss Penny knelt next to me. "Oh Josie." She held my arms in her hands and looked me in the eye. "Why ever did you kick him? That is so out of character for you."

I started to shake.

"Oh dear," she said. "Sit down here." She put me in a chair and she got me a drink from the water cooler. Then she took her handkerchief, wet it with more cool water, and put it on the back of my neck. "Are you going to be all right?"

"Uh-huh," I mumbled. The wet cloth felt good on my neck.

Mr. Springfield stepped out of his office. Looking at Billy and me he said, "What's this?"

After MP explained, Mr. Springfield said, "Josie, I never thought I'd see the day when you would be here for kicking someone. Come in my office."

Inside the principal's office, I told Mr. Springfield how Billy had squirted ink on my blouse and called my father a slacker.

"I see." The principal telephoned my parents. He seemed to be listening more than talking. Finally he said, "Joe, someone should come down here and take Josie home." He turned to me. "Send Billy in please and wait outside."

Billy had his turn telling his side of the story. Afterward, I sat as far away from him as I could while we waited for our parents to arrive.

"You're going to be sorry," he threatened.

No kidding, I thought.

When Mother arrived she gasped. "You're so pale." She felt my forehead. "And clammy." She looked at Billy and then back at me. "You kicked him?"

I nodded. *What are my parents going to do? I've never been in trouble like this.* Now I was feeling sick.

"What did he do?" Mother asked.

"He called Daddy a slacker."

She stared at me. "What happened to your blouse?"

"He squirted ink on me. Then he called Daddy—"

"Did not," Billy said.

Mother cut Billy a sharp look and sat next to me. "Girls don't fight," she whispered.

I was in so much trouble.

When Mrs. Detwiler arrived, she clutched her hands to her bosom as if she were Theda Bara and draped herself around Billy. "Oh my poor boy! Did *she* do this to you? Which leg is it?" Without even looking at Billy's injury, she turned on Mother. "What is the matter with your children? First that infernal gun, and now this! His leg could be broken! He could be permanently lame!" She stood up and shook her finger at my mother. "You'll pay the doctors' bills on this!" Mrs. Detwiler stomped into Mr. Springfield's office and slammed the door. Even still, we could hear her shout, "I want that girl expelled!"

Expelled? I started feeling woozy.

Someone said, "Ethel, she's going to faint. She's whiter than her blouse."

Mother pushed my head down below my knees. At least the buzzing stopped in my head.

Mr. Springfield appeared at the door and waved all of us in, but I stayed curled up across two chairs. The school secretary mopped my brow with Miss Penny's cold handkerchief.

I could hear my mother in Mr. Springfield's office. She told the principal how Billy had been harassing me since the beginning of school. The ruined blouse was just another example of his bullying. And now all of this was making me physically ill.

Of course Mrs. Detwiler interrupted, saying it was all a pack of lies. She was furious that Mother would worry about a shirt when her poor son's leg might be broken. He might have problems for the rest of his life.

My mother said, "We can only hope . . . "

Someone choked. I think it was Mr. Springfield.

" . . . that it's nothing serious," Mother finished.

If I moved a bit on the chairs, I could see Mr. Springfield. He held his chin and seemed to be thinking. Then he folded his hands on the desk and said, "Children have to learn to get along. We all have to learn to work together and put differences aside—especially in times like these." He paused.

Mrs. Detwiler nodded and gave my mother a hollow-hearted smile.

"But as we discussed in August when you registered Billy for school—" Mr. Springfield peered over the top of his glasses—"fighting is a serious infraction of our school rules and there will be consequences."

Mrs. Detwiler stiffened. "She kicked my son. He's the victim here."

"As I see it, Billy provoked Josie. But there will be consequences for both students. Josie, do you feel well enough to come in now?" asked Mr. Springfield.

I went in.

Mr. Springfield spoke to Billy and me. "Do either of you have anything you want to say?"

I knew this was an invitation to apologize. "I'm sorry. I'm sorry I kicked Billy. I hope his leg is not broken."

"Good," said Mr. Springfield. "Josie, you have three days of detention, and it starts tomorrow after school. I hope you have learned a lesson here. And for now, I think you need to go home with your mother."

I'm not expelled! I wanted to jump for joy.

Mr. Springfield turned to Billy. "Anything you wish to say, young man?"

Billy didn't answer.

"You have detentions too," Mr. Springfield said.

Mrs. Detwiler started to fuss, but the principal put up his hand as if to say, "Stop." "According to his school records, this is not the first time Billy has been to the principal's office for some sort of problem getting along with classmates. Detentions start tomorrow after school."

Mother stood up. "I'm sorry for all this trouble. Let's hope this is the end of it. Mr. Winslow and I support your decision." Mother shook hands with Mr. Springfield and turned to Mrs. Detwiler. "Send us the medical bills." She paused. "And I know you will take care of the blouse problem."

Mother held her arm around my shoulder on the way home. "We'll soak that stain in milk overnight. You know," she said, laughing a little, "when I told you this morning to be brave, this was not what I had in mind."

Over a cup of chamomile tea, I learned that Dad had insisted Mr. Springfield give me the same punishment as Billy. Dad did not want to give Mrs. Detwiler any chance to complain about privilege. Darn that woman. This was unfair.

CHAPTER NINE

SPANISH INFLUENZA

The next morning, Mother checked the ink stain. Only a little of it had come out. Her next plan was to soak the stain in lemon juice. As she squeezed a lemon on the reamer and grumbled about Mrs. Detwiler, Mother pushed so hard the lemon split.

That afternoon I served detention with Miss Penny. No Billy. I had to write a hundred punishment sentences: "Students need to get along with each other." When I was almost done, Miss Penny asked me about the map of my father's store I had drawn for homework.

I shrugged. "I noticed it was missing from the bulletin board."

"I wonder where it is." Miss Penny picked up a neat stack of papers and started to leaf through them. Then she checked her grade book. "There's an A here for the assignment." Miss Penny smiled. "I'm sure it will turn up." She put the grade book on top of the papers. "Josie, you're not too old to help me wash blackboards, are you?"

It had never occurred to me I might be outgrowing washing blackboards. "Yes . . . No . . . I mean I'm glad to help you, Miss Penny."

"Thank you, Josie. And when you are done, we can both go home." Miss Penny closed the windows and adjusted the shades while I finished the boards.

We walked out of school together. "See you Monday, Josie." She waved.

I waved bye back. I loved Miss Penny.

∾

Saturday morning I checked the stain on my blouse. The ink was still visible. Mother tried oxalic acid. I wondered if the acid would eat the fabric.

Thanks to Billy, I was not allowed to go to the library today. But that did not prevent me from delivering papers.

As I came through the backyard after finishing the papers, I could see the clothesline hanging limp and a sheet dragging on the grass. I heard a commotion in the store and ran to see what was wrong.

Tiny peeked through the screen door. "Daddy's choking."

I yanked open the door, nearly knocking my sister over.

Dad coughed and laughed so hard he banged his hand on the pharmacy counter, rattling the medicine bottles. Mother was trying to pound him on the back. "Joe! Hold still!"

I was scared. But he was finally able to get his breath.

Dad's face was bright red. He cleared his throat and handed Mother a newspaper.

She read the headline: "Kiss with Care."

Kissing? This could be embarrassing.

"New York City's Commissioner of Health officially advises against kissing . . . " Mother held the back of her hand up to her nose and turned red. She was trying not to laugh. "No kissing . . . except through a handkerchief . . . a simple means of evading Spanish influenza. Authorities say the handkerchief kiss should be brought into vogue at once."

Dad pulled his handkerchief out of his pocket. He flicked it open and draped it across his face like surgeon's mask. With each word, the handkerchief poofed out. "Ethel, my dear, it's time for a big smooch!"

Oh no! He's not going to —

He did! Dad gave Mother a kiss right there in the store with the ridiculous handkerchief on his face!

Then Dad folded up his handkerchief and said, "The man's an idiot."

Dad quit fooling around and started counting empty prescription bottles. "Josie, I'd like you to collect used bottles when you deliver papers. We need them back and ready to use in case Dr. Copeland is wrong."

ॐ

First thing Sunday morning, I checked the stain on my blouse. Oxalic acid took a little more of it out, but not enough. Mother said we would wash it one more time and see if the sun could bleach it any more.

Later that afternoon, Grace came over. Once we were in my bedroom and out of earshot of grown-ups, Grace blurted, "You will never guess what's in this book!"

She had checked out a copy of *The Wind in the Willows* yesterday at the library. It was the book MP was reading to us in class.

"Rat and Mole argue about who is going to row the boat, and Rat gets knocked down." Grace turned to a page she had marked. "Rat's afraid Mole will capsize their little boat and yells, 'Stop it, you *silly*...'" Grace looked around checking for grown-ups and whispered, '*ass!*'"

My jaw dropped. Grace pointed to the forbidden word.

"This is a children's book!" I whispered. "Do you think MP will read this part aloud? Will she say—A-blank-blank?"

I couldn't say the actual words. We both knew we'd get our mouths washed out with soap for saying curse words. Nice girls didn't curse.

"Do you think she knows . . . that it's in there? Should we tell her?"

Grace shrugged.

Tiny came in our room. "What are you doing?"

Grace and I said at the same time, "Nothing."

Grace left the book with me so we could take turns reading. After I got in bed, I started from the beginning and read to the part Grace showed me. The next thing I knew I was thinking, "What silly ass is banging on the door with a boat oar?" Then I woke up and realized someone was banging on the store door and shouting.

"Mr. Winslow! Mr. Winslow! Doctor Fagan needs you! It's my mother!" It was Tony Santorini from our class.

I heard Dad on the stairs, and Mother called out the window, "He's coming, Tony."

Gram threw on her robe and hurried downstairs with Mother to help. Through the open window I could hear the shop bell jingle. Dad was letting Tony in the store. Tiny and I watched by our bedroom window. In no time, Dad and Tony were hurrying up Raritan Avenue towards Tony's house.

"Is Tony's mother having another baby?" I asked when Gram came back to bed. Doc Fagan often asked Dad or Gram to help him deliver babies.

"No. It sounds like Mrs. Santorini might have the flu," she said.

"Gram, does she have pneumonia?"

"We'll know tomorrow. Try to sleep, Josie."

CHAPTER TEN

BLITZCATARRH

"Josie, that stain isn't any better," Mother said the next morning at breakfast. "Mrs. Detwiler is going to have to replace the blouse."

"So, are you going to tell her?" Gram asked.

Mother replied, "Just as soon as . . . "

Dad came in the back door. He had been at the Santorinis' all night. Dried blood stained the front of his shirt.

"How is she?" Mother asked.

"Barely alive. The priest is there now." Dad ran his fingers through his hair. "Poor woman was coughing up blood. She turned blue."

Mother offered him coffee.

"Keep it warm. I need to wash up."

Mother pointed at my cereal bowl. That meant get busy or I'd be late for school.

Gram said that only last Thursday Mrs. Santorini had brought the socks she had knitted to the Red Cross Women's meeting and she seemed perfectly fine.

Dad came back, buttoning a clean shirt.

"Daddy, could Tony's mother die?" I asked. "When the priest comes, doesn't that mean . . . ?"

My father sat at the kitchen table. "Yes, many times that's what it means, Josie." He sipped his coffee.

"But it's just influenza," Mother said. "How could she be so sick so fast?"

"I don't know." Dad yawned. "She's young. She's healthy. She should have been able to fight it off."

Tony wasn't in school today. Neither was Billy. I started to worry again that Billy might be in the hospital, but when I told Grace she said, "Don't you think that crank, Mrs. Detwiler, would have complained to your parents by now if he was really hurt?" I could count on Grace to be sensible.

After lunch Miss Penny read aloud from *The Wind in the Willows*. She was near the part where Rat and Mole were in the boat. Grace and I kept sneaking looks at each other. Would MP say it? Would she say "silly A-blank-blank"?

Miss Penny stopped and looked at the clock. Closing the book, she said, "We'll pick up here tomorrow."

Fiddlesticks! We had to wait.

≈

After school I served my second detention in MP's classroom. It had been about fifteen minutes when Principal Springfield came into the room. "Go on home now, Josie," he said.

As I gathered my books, Mr. Springfield whispered something to Miss Penny. She gasped and covered her mouth with her hands. Whatever he told her, it wasn't good. What would make MP gasp? My thoughts came out of my mouth before I could stop them. "Did Tony's mother die?"

MP looked surprised and said softly, "Yes."

≈

When I got home, Gram was in the backyard taking down laundry.

"Gram, Tony's mother . . . " I paused because I didn't want to say the words.

"She died this afternoon." Gram shook her head in that slow, "I can't believe it" way. "She had only been sick since Saturday."

Influenza is contagious. "What about Tony? And his brothers and sister?" *And Daddy,* I thought, but I didn't say it aloud.

Gram flicked a bug off Dad's shirt. "Tony's father has the flu. It's probably only a matter of time until they all come down with it."

"Was it Spanish flu?" I asked.

"We can only hope it's not." She picked up the laundry basket, and we headed upstairs.

In the kitchen, I could smell chicken soup. Jars of soup cooled next to the stove. They would be for Tony's family. Another pot of chicken simmered on the back burner. That would be our dinner. Gram said we'd be having chicken and "Irish" dumplings, wheatless dumplings Gram had concocted from potatoes.

Dinner that night was quiet. The poor Santorini family was on everyone's mind. Finally, Dad asked, "How was school?"

"Billy was absent again," I said.

Dad raised his eyebrows and nodded. "And detention?"

"Mr. Springfield let me go early. I guess because of Mrs. Santorini."

Like every other night, Dad read the newspaper and drank coffee. "There are eight thousand cases of flu at Camp Devens in Massachusetts. That's an astounding number."

"Do you think they got it wrong?" Mother asked. "Eight thousand—that's more people than we have in Highland Park."

"It just makes me wonder," Dad said, "why New York City is reporting only twenty-three cases, and they say the cases are mild. Donna Santorini's case"—Dad stopped and took a sip of his coffee—"was in no way mild."

⇜

At bedtime I folded my arms behind my head and stared at the ceiling. I could hear Tiny turning pages in *Raggedy Ann,* pretending to read.

"Josie, do you want to see the pictures?" my sister asked.

"No, thank you. I'll just listen." I watched the sheer curtains wave back and forth in the breeze created by the fan.

Gram and Tiny took turns reading. Mother came in and gave us each a kiss. "Good night, Pharmacy Girl," she whispered to me.

"Good night, Mother."

Dad leaned in the doorway. "Good night, ladies." He blew us kisses.

We blew kisses back. "'Night, Daddy."

As I lay in bed, I thought about how Tony had come to the store in the middle of the night. I wished it were last night again. Then Tony's mother would still be alive. She could still give Tony and his brothers and sister good night kisses. And read to them. And come get them from school if they were in trouble. Tears ran out of the corners of my eyes and rolled down my cheeks into my ears.

⇜

In the morning, the ironing board was already up, and Gram was sprinkling water on yesterday's clean wash.

"Josie," Gram said, handing me a still-warm handkerchief, "you need to return this to Miss Penny." It was the one MP had lent me when Billy made me cry. Then Gram showed the middy blouse to Mother. The ink stain was still hopelessly gray. "Is there any point in ironing this?" she asked.

Mother looked at me as she put oatmeal in my bowl.

I shook my head no. Weeks of delivering papers just to contribute to the ragbag. *I hate Billy Detwiler.*

At the start of school, Miss Penny read the Twenty-Third Psalm, as she always did. We stood for the Pledge of Allegiance and sang "America," as we always did. But this morning Miss Penny added a moment of silence for Tony's mother.

Concentrating on schoolwork was difficult. I couldn't stop thinking about Mrs. Santorini. And how Dad had been in the same room with her. Even when Miss Penny read *The Wind in the Willows*, I couldn't pay attention.

Grace leaned over across the aisle and poked me, "She didn't say it!"

"What?"

Grace whispered, "Goose! She said, 'Silly *goose!*'"

Blast.

That afternoon was my last detention. I asked MP about Billy. Was he really hurt? Was he in the hospital? But Miss Penny did not know.

ॐ

No detention today. Yay! On the way home, Grace and I hopped over puddles from this afternoon's rain. Suddenly she stopped short like she always did when she had something important to say. She asked me if I thought it was a coincidence that it was raining on the day of Mrs. Santorini's funeral. I knew what she meant. It was as if the whole world was sad and angels were crying.

Upstairs, Mother and Gram were having tea and talking about Mrs. Santorini's funeral. They said only Tony and his brothers were there. Mr. Santorini and Tony's sister, Maria, were too sick with influenza to come to the service. Tony's grandparents were there too. Gram said it was so heartbreaking to see Mrs. Santorini's mother and father grieving over their "child."

Dad worked through dinner. I took a plate of food down to the store. Doctor Fagan was there taking inventory of things in his doctor's bag. "Aspirin . . . phenacitin . . . cough syrup . . . codeine . . . citrate of magnesia. I think I'm set." As he took empty prescription bottles from his bag he said, "Seventy people died in Boston from the flu — in one day. And there are cases now right here in New Jersey at Camp Dix."

"Let me guess," Dad said. "Authorities think it's just old-fashioned flu. So, do you think this is old-fashioned influenza?"

Doctor Fagan loosened his tie. "Patients say the headache is like someone hitting your head with a hammer. Although some of the cases appear mild in comparison to Mrs. Santorini, I think we are in for some rough seas on this. I'm not convinced this is the usual flu."

≈

In the morning, Grace waited for me at the bottom of our stairs. "Josie, I thought about this all night. We've got to do something good for the Liberty Loan drive!"

"We are," I said. Miss Penny had been talking in civics about what we could do for the Fourth Liberty Loan. "I thought we could be in the parade again, for the rally."

"We need to buy bonds ourselves! We need to raise money."

Grace started to tell me about her plan, but I had to drag her along so we wouldn't be late for school. Grace said she'd read about girls having a lemonade stand and raising over ten dollars. That would be enough for two books of War Savings Stamps.

"Was that ten dollars the profit or their receipts?" I asked.

Grace stopped walking. She was thinking.

"Lemons and paper cups will cost money. And sugar. Sugar might not be easy," I reminded her.

Grace bit her lip. "We'll think of something."

༭

On the way home from school, Grace stopped in the store with me.

"Good, you're home," Gram said. "We need to wash prescription bottles. Grace, you can help if you want. It's like washing baby bottles. Or canning. You'll need to know this one day."

The dishpan with the bottles was upstairs waiting. Basically, this was washing dishes, only we used a bottlebrush to remove any caked medicine from the bottom of the bottle. Scrub. Rinse. Look carefully. Scrub again. Scrub and rinse until there wasn't a trace of old medicine. We let Tiny scrub some of the bottles, but then we gave them a second scrubbing to get what she missed. We put the clean bottles in a hot water bath on the stove where they would be sterilized in boiling water.

"That's a small batch," Gram said. "We're going to need more."

"I know," I said. "I'm collecting bottles on Saturday."

"Jo-o-seee," Mother called from the foot of the back stairs. "Your father needs you to take this prescription over to Mrs. Meyer's."

Grace left, and Mother gave me a small brown paper sack with several bottles of medicine. "There's influenza at the house, so just leave these on the front porch. Doctor Fagan is expecting you." Mother held my chin in her hand and looked me straight in the eye. "Don't go inside, you hear me? Use your scooter, it's faster."

For the second night in a row, Doc Fagan and Dad worked in the pharmacy at dinnertime. Dad had me bring two dinners down. He wanted to make sure Doc Fagan ate to keep up his resistance too. As I left the store Doc Fagan said, "God, Joe. This flu hits so fast—it's as if people were struck by lightning. No wonder the Germans call it *blitzcatarrh*."

CHAPTER ELEVEN

SPIES AND LEMONADE

By Friday, Billy was back in school and in his glory. A crowd of boys hovered around him.

"So, Billy, where were you all week?" Fred asked.

"Not with the Boy Scouts, that's for sure," Billy mocked. "I bet things were pretty tame around here. Ha! You are a bunch of milk and water babies." Billy pulled a pamphlet out of his back pocket. "Listen, Fred. You and your pal, Tony — Where's Tony anyway?

Everyone looked awkward. Didn't Billy know about Tony's mother? Would anyone tell him?

But before anyone could say anything, Billy kept going. "You two, and the rest of you slackers, should quit Boy Scouts and join up with the Anti-Yellow Dog League." Billy waved the pamphlet in the boys' faces. "That's what I did. Now I get to do some real work to beat the Germans. We report spies and slackers to the authorities."

No one said a word.

"What's the matter with you? Don't you want to catch spies?" Billy scowled at the small crowd of classmates. "What an unpatriotic bunch! You're lucky you're kids, or I'd probably have to report all of you for being yellow."

"We're not yellow." It was out of my mouth before I could stop it. Too late, I clapped my hand over my mouth. Oh fiddlesticks!

"Who said that?" Billy scanned our faces. He stopped at Grace and me. "It was a girl, and it sounded like you, Pharmacy Girl." He leaned in, staring.

Fred stepped in between us. "They're girls. Leave 'em alone. Hey, I heard you cut those detentions the principal gave you."

"Some things are more important than measly detentions," Billy said, still glaring at me. "My cousin was drafted, and we went to Camp Upton to see him before he ships out. I got to see bayonet practice." Billy made as if he was stabbing Fred in the gut.

Fred put his arms out so Billy couldn't reach him.

"You probably can't stand the sight of blood, let alone someone's guts spilling out. I bet you'd faint," Billy taunted.

Now Fred backed off. So did everyone else. Mr. Springfield grabbed Billy by the back of the collar. "The only blood we're going to see on this playground is from scraped knees. Now if you will be so kind as to come to my office, you'll be spending recess with me for the foreseeable future."

Once they were inside the school, everyone howled. But I kept my thoughts to myself. My heart was still pounding.

☙

When I got home, Mother was in the pharmacy typing notes for me to put with the newspapers. "Please leave empty prescription bottles on your doorstep. Josie will collect them. Thank you." Mother pulled the paper out of the typewriter. "Are you hungry? Wash up while I make us a milk shake. We need to use the last of the peach ice cream. It's starting to crystalize, and I don't want it to go to waste."

Crystalized ice cream wasn't bad to eat. It just didn't feel creamy like you expected. Mother and Dad thought ice cream and milk were wholesome foods. The milk and eggs in ice cream were good for you. And the sugar was good for energy. Although sometimes I worried that eating ice cream wasn't very patriotic, throwing it away would be worse.

In between sips, I cut apart the bottle notices and tried to tell my parents about Billy. I slurped the last drops of milk shake through my straw.

"Slurping," Mother said, "is bad manners."

"Sorry. Billy Detwiler's back."

"Do you know why he skipped detentions?" Mother asked.

"He was at Camp Upton visiting a cousin."

"Upton's under quarantine," Dad said. "Maybe the Detwilers will be lucky and won't come down with the flu."

≈

Saturday, Grace and I made our usual trip to the library. This time Janet and Winnie came, too. Ever since the librarian had shown us the Ruth Fielding books, we were crazy to read them. Ruth Fielding was bold and courageous and had adventures we could only dream of.

On our way home, we stopped at Van Drusen's Pharmacy. Dad had known Mr. Van Drusen for years and did not mind if I patronized his store. It was also a favorite haunt for Rutgers students and was usually busy on Saturday afternoons. My friends and I agreed that one day it was going to be awfully fun to have boys treat us to ice cream sundaes. But for now, that had to wait. None of us were allowed to even talk to college boys because they were so much older.

Over our sodas, we discussed our plans to raise money for the Liberty Loan. Everyone liked Grace's idea to sell lemonade. Janet's brothers had built a lemonade stand that we could use. I said Dad might donate paper cups or at least only charge us his cost.

"We have recipes for large quantities of lemonade at the store," I volunteered. "Our biggest problem will be getting sugar."

"What if each of us donates a cup of sugar?" Grace suggested, and we all agreed we'd ask our mothers to help us.

"Winnie, if you help me, we can decorate the lemonade stand and make posters advertising the sale," said Janet.

"I'll get the lemons," Grace chimed in.

"If we have the sale just before the Liberty Loan starts, we might get a jump on things and do better," I said.

We had just started talking about how much to charge for lemonade when Janet said, "Uh-oh" and ducked down, covering her forehead with her hand.

"What? What's wrong?" Winnie turned to look.

"Shush," Janet whispered. "Turn around."

"Detwiler," mouthed Winnie.

We all kept our heads down and pretended to be busy talking.

Mrs. Detwiler strode past us to the pharmacy counter where we heard her ask for aspirin and Dover's Powders.

Grace made a face. "Dover's," she muttered. "We know what *that's* for."

"Dover's? What's that?" Winnie whispered in my ear.

"You know, it makes you . . . go." I said. I didn't dare look at Grace or I would have burst out laughing, and Mrs. Detwiler would notice us.

The next thing we knew, the glass and wood frame front door slammed open and Billy burst into the store. Through the store window, I could see two boys. One was shaking his fist, but I couldn't hear what he was saying.

Billy walked over to his mother as if nothing was wrong, but his hair was a mess, and he was breathing hard as if he had been running.

"Tuck in your shirt, Billy," his mother instructed.

"I want some Coca-Cola," he demanded, keeping a lookout over his shoulder at the doorway.

The boys were gone. But two Rutgers students came in and the girls at the next table waved and called them over.

Billy blanched. "Never mind," he said to his mother. "I don't want a drink. Hurry up. Let's go home."

"Make up your mind." His mother sounded irritated.

As the college boys sat with their girlfriends, we couldn't help but hear their conversation. "If I catch those kids . . . calling us slackers. The insolent little toughs barked at us, and one of them said he was one of the Anti-Yellow Dog League. He wanted to see our draft cards."

One of the girls shushed him. "Keep your voice down," she cautioned.

We all looked at each other. "Do you think he's talking about Billy?" Janet whispered.

As Billy and his mother headed toward the door, Billy reached his arm around his back and made a rude gesture so his mother couldn't see. But we did.

"Hey! Isn't that . . . ?" The college student shouted as he jumped up in the booth. "I'd think your mother would have taught you better manners."

Mrs. Detwiler stopped dead in her tracks, turned, and glared.

My chocolate ice cream soda suddenly felt like hot coals burning in my stomach.

"He's a slacker, Momma," Billy said. "He wouldn't show me his draft card."

"Well, maybe he will show *me*." As she walked over to the students, Mrs. Detwiler pulled a small badge out of her purse and showed it to the college students. "American Protective League. I have the authority to ask you to show me your draft card."

Both Rutgers students took out their wallets.

This was so humiliating. I wanted to throw something at Mrs. Detwiler. But I didn't dare. It would only make things worse.

"Strong, able-bodied young men like you should have quit school and joined up," Mrs. Detwiler accused.

"But they are both in the Students' Army Training Corps," one of the girls said in the boys' defense.

Don't argue with her, I thought. It's useless.

"And one would think nice girls would not want to be seen with cowards." Like her son, Mrs. Detwiler went for the last shot.

Was no one safe from her terrifying tongue?

On Sunday, church seemed empty. We prayed for our soldiers and the end of the war. We prayed for the influenza victims. Grace's mother said the number of sick people needing prayers was the longest she had ever heard.

As we left church, Grace's mother stopped, just as Grace did when she was thinking. "What if you girls had your lemonade sale here on the lawn by the church? You'd need permission from Pastor McElroy."

Grace gave me a "what do you think?" look.

"We don't have any better ideas right now," I said. "Let's ask Winnie and Janet."

CHAPTER TWELVE:

One for the Money, Two for the Show, Three to Get Ready — Oh No!

Come Monday, Miss Penny announced that the Liberty Loan organizers wanted schools to participate in oratory contests. The winner from each school would make a speech at the upcoming bond rally.

"Who remembers what a Four-Minute Speech is?" MP asked.

I had heard my first Four-Minute Speech at the Strand Theatre on Albany Street last spring when Grace and I went to a motion picture. I raised my hand. "Volunteers go to public gatherings to make short speeches to help drum up support for the Liberty Loan."

"That's right, Josie, and that is exactly what we are going to do," Miss Penny said.

Grace gave a little groan and put her head down on her desk. The boys were louder. Billy came right out and booed! I thought, not *another* speech. One speech a year was enough, and I had already given one. Maybe if I got laryngitis I wouldn't have to make a speech.

Miss Penny took the moaning in stride. "This will be fun," she said. "I know you can do a bang-up job!"

"Send me 'over there'!" Fred called out. "Send me to the trenches! Anything but making a speech!"

Miss Penny tried not to laugh. "I knew my students were patriotic! Fred, you may be too young to go to France, but you are not too young to do something good here at home." Then Miss Penny dropped her voice. "You know, class, the more we can do here at home, the sooner we can end the war, and the sooner our soldiers can come home."

Everyone got quiet. We all knew Miss Penny's fiancé was fighting in France.

Fred broke the silence. "You win, Miss Penny. But I want to give my speech first so I can get it over with!"

"That's the spirit, Fred!" Miss Penny cheered. "Now, the best speakers from each class will give their Four-Minute talks at a Liberty Loan assembly we will have here at school. For now, work on writing your speeches and practicing." Miss Penny wrote "Speeches" on the side blackboard. Underneath she wrote "#1 Fred." She tapped the board with her chalk. "Sign up so we know when your turn will be. Now let's think of some ideas you might use."

৶

The next day, Janet and Winnie caught up to us outside of school. "We can get the sugar," Janet said.

Grace nodded, "Me too, and my mother talked to Pastor McElroy. He gave us permission to have the lemonade sale on the church lawn."

"How much sugar do we need, Josie?" Winnie asked.

"If we each contribute a cup of sugar, we can serve fifty people. If we charge a nickel a glass, that's $2.50."

Two dollars and fifty cents? I hit my forehead with the heel of my hand. *Dummy!* "It's not enough. Divided four ways, that would be less than a dollar for each of us. And we haven't even subtracted for any expenses. We have to charge more," I said. "Ten cents times fifty would earn us five dollars."

"Grace, how did those girls you read about earn ten dollars?" asked Winnie.

"We'll just have to sell more lemonade," Grace answered.

"One hundred cups of lemonade at ten cents would get us the ten dollars," I said. "But that will mean we each have to contribute two cups of sugar."

Principal Springfield rang the school bell. Maybe it was my imagination, but it seemed to me I heard a lot of coughing as we crowded into school.

⁂

"Where's Mother?" I asked Dad as I came in the store.

"She's with your grandmother visiting some of Dr. Fagan's patients who need nursing. Your sister is next door with Mrs. Senker."

It bothered me that Mother and Gram exposed themselves to influenza. They could catch it.

Dad brought the newspapers and what looked like a bundle of new Liberty Loan posters into the store. He opened the posters on the counter.

The first poster showed a beautiful woman depicting Liberty. An American flag unfurled behind her, she pointed out to sea as if she were pointing to Europe. Beneath her, an American gun crew loaded ammunition into the big guns of a battleship. It was easy to see how Liberty Loan money would be spent.

Another poster showed a mean-looking German soldier with a bloody bayonet. Behind him, a town was in flames. Everything was burning, including a church. It made my skin crawl to think the Germans would burn even churches.

⁂

On Wednesday Flossie fell asleep on her desk. Poor Flossie. Billy no longer sat right behind her, but he could still see, and of course, as soon as he figured out Flossie was asleep he announced it to the whole class. "Flossie's sleeping," he taunted in a singsong voice. "And she's drooling."

Classmates giggled. Flossie woke up and looked around the room as if she didn't know where she was. She wiped her mouth with her shirt cuff. Everyone stared at her. Flossie's face was flushed and her eyes looked glassy.

Miss Penny felt Flossie's forehead. "Oh dear, you are burning up. Do you feel all right?"

Flossie shook her head no, and MP sent Flossie to the office to go home.

Four classmates were already absent. Tony was still not back. Flossie made number five. I wondered if Flossie had Spanish influenza. Maybe we all did.

After school Winnie, Janet, Grace, and I took our lemonade sale posters to different stores on Raritan Avenue. As I came home, I could see the Liberty Loan posters in our store windows. There was still space for the lemonade sale poster.

"Hello," I called out automatically. When my father didn't answer, I realized he was waiting on a customer and Mother was not in the store again. "I'm sorry. I did not mean to interrupt," I said.

The customer turned.

Cat's whiskers! It was Mrs. Detwiler. I think she sneered at me.

Dad continued, "With the Spanish influenza so prevalent, I can only sell you one bottle of aspirin. Deliveries are behind because of the flu. I need to ration my stock, but this should last you and Billy for a while."

She harrumphed like a hippopotamus, paid Dad, and left the store.

I told Dad she had been buying aspirin and flu supplies on Saturday at Van Drusen's and how she demanded to see draft cards of some Rutgers students.

"I wonder what her friends in the American Protective League would say if they knew she was hoarding and still checking draft cards — especially since the organization isn't officially taking women members now." He picked up two long brown-paper tubes and set them aside on the shelves behind the soda fountain. "Here are your paper cups for Sunday."

"Thanks, Daddy. How do you like our poster?" I showed Dad the poster with Uncle Sam's boot stepping on a lemon. The lemon was wearing what was supposed to be a German helmet with the spike on top.

"Squish the Kaiser! Nicely done." Dad put the poster in the remaining spot in the window. "How was school?"

"Flossie went home sick this morning. That makes five absent."

"So, how's that speech going?" he asked.

I almost choked. *I hadn't thought about the speech since Monday.* I started coughing. Dad asked if I was all right. But I kept clearing my throat because I had swallowed wrong. He gave me some syrup and water to sip. *I had been too busy working on the lemonade sale.* Maybe I could use some of my election speech over again. Four minutes? That's forever. How on earth am I going to do this?

&

The next day I received a letter from the *Home News*.

"Dear Paper Carriers, We hope that once again we can count on our family of paperboys to contribute to the upcoming Liberty Loan Drive. The money you earn delivering papers can be put to good use to help our soldiers 'over there' who are making the world safe for Democracy. Buying a Liberty Bond is patriotic, and it makes good financial sense because when the war is over, your bond will be worth more for the reason that your bond is gaining interest. By purchasing a war bond, you will be saving lives and saving for your own future. We know we can count on you to do the right thing. Sincerely . . . "

"The paper wants me to buy a Liberty Bond." I handed the letter to my father. "I'm trying to buy enough Thrift Stamps with the lemonade money to buy a War

Savings Stamp, and now the publisher wants me to buy a Liberty *Bond* with my paper money? That's fifty dollars!"

"Just do your best, Josie. That's all anyone can ask," Dad said.

The Liberty Loan wouldn't end until mid-October. Maybe there was time. I looked at the second page of the letter. It was a flyer with a list of how our money would be used to help win the war. My meager contribution would never be enough to buy a bomb, but it might buy some bandages.

Doctor Fagan came in the store. "The paper says flu's spread all over the country and federal and military officials are talking to the Red Cross about what they can do."

"I saw that," Dad said. "New England's thinking about curtailing public gatherings."

"Good luck," remarked Doc Fagan. "With the Fourth Liberty Loan about to start? How are health officials going to stop parades and rallies to raise money?" The doctor helped himself to a cup of coffee at the soda fountain. "Although they should."

Dad grimaced. "Be careful what you say. You never know when the APL will show up."

APL? The American Protective League. Mrs. Detwiler could, and would, report anything that sounded anti-government.

"I know. They're pestering me to join. But with this epidemic, they've backed off." He sipped the coffee. "This epidemic . . . I'll tell you, Joe . . . this epidemic is different. Why is it that the healthiest age group, young adults—men your age—is the same group so stricken with Spanish influenza?"

There was a gnawing feeling in my stomach.

"The Red Cross is sending ambulances and drivers to Camp Dix because all the trucks have been sent to France," Dr. Fagan said. "Now the medical staff only has wagons and mules to transport the sick . . . and the dead. I'm told even the mules were exhausted and needed relief." The doctor handed Dad a short stack of prescriptions to fill.

Dad separated the slips on the pharmacy counter. "You know about the girls' lemonade sale on Sunday?"

"I saw the posters." Doc Fagan made a tsking sound. "Public gathering . . . I don't know . . . "

NO! Is he thinking we should cancel the lemonade sale because of the flu? I rushed over to Dad and Doc Fagan. "I have to do the lemonade sale! I promised my friends. I can't go back on them now."

"Whoa," said Dad. "Take it easy."

"How will I earn enough money to buy War Savings Stamps?" I asked, trying to sound reasonable. "People will think I'm unpatriotic. My friends will think I'm a slacker."

"The girls would be outside." Doc Fagan rubbed his chin. "Not like being in a crowded trolley or a classroom." But he still had a worried look on his face.

"Daddy, please say yes," I begged. "I have to do this!"

"Let's see what tomorrow brings."

It was not really a "no," but it also wasn't really a "yes."

જી

The next day, I put strips of white adhesive tape on the bottoms of custard cups and wrote "Winslow" on the tape. We were giving more food away. The Red Cross was collecting custard, jellies, flowers, and magazines for soldiers at Camp Raritan who had come down with influenza. We were sending jellies, as they would keep better than custard.

At dinner Mother talked about her trip to the Red Cross Room. "We will be going through closets again for donations," she said to Gram. "Next week they're collecting linens to send to hospitals in France. They're calling this next drive a 'shower,' like a wedding shower or a baby shower."

"Doesn't seem quite the same thing, does it?" Gram said.

"You should see what the Liberty Loan committees have done with the store windows," Mother said. "The Young Department Store has a mannequin dressed like an older woman—a mother—looking at a picture of a soldier. She's holding a letter saying he was killed in action. A banner says, 'She gave her all. Won't you lend?' So heartbreaking." Mother shivered as if she had a chill. "And Wolfson's Department Store has a display of uniforms, insignia, and equipment fighting men will need—even two stacks of guns are on display in the window."

"Shall we clean out the linen closet tomorrow and see if we have anything for the shower?" Gram asked.

"Let's put a notice about collecting linens in the paper," Mother said. "People can leave their donations with us, and we'll take them to New Brunswick. I can telephone the paper in the morning."

And then Mother dropped a bombshell. "Josie, your father talked to me about the lemonade sale. He thinks it's risky. You could all catch influenza."

My heart skipped a beat. "He said we would wait and see."

"I know. He told me that too."

"We would be outside. It's harder to catch the flu if you are outside."

Gram and Mother both looked sympathetic.

"I don't want my friends to think I'm a slacker. Please don't say no. My friends are counting on me."

"It's up to your father," Mother said.

"Gram, you took soup to Tony's house, and you didn't catch it," I said. "And Mother, you've been visiting the sick too. You go inside and are exposed to the germs. You take the risk to help others."

"But we're adults," said Mother.

"Yes, and adults your age are just the ones getting hit the hardest with the flu! Doc Fagan said so!"

Gram reached over to pat my hand. "There, there, Josie. Things will work out."

I pulled my hand away and banged my fist on the kitchen table, "No! It's not fair! Mother, you said how awful it is to lose a child. Well, it's just as awful to lose a parent!" I was crying now. "I don't want any of us to get Spanish influenza and die!"

"Who's dying?" Tiny asked.

"No one," Gram said, reaching over to pull Tiny on her lap.

Mother moved closer to me. She put her arm around my shoulder and pulled me close. "No one's going to die here," she whispered. "Drink some milk . . . we need to keep our strength up if we are going to fight off the flu and the Germans."

The screen door squeaked.

"What's going on here?" It was Dad.

Mother explained as Dad sat at the kitchen table.

"Josie, there's no hiding that fact that the flu is bad this year." Dad leaned closer. "It's so bad the government is postponing the draft call for October to try to stop the spread of influenza in our army camps. That's a very unusual thing to do in the middle of a war."

"They actually postponed the draft call?" Mother sounded amazed.

Dad nodded. "And the Senate is thinking of spending a million dollars to fight the flu because it is so widespread."

"Daddy, that's all the more reason we should raise money for our soldiers," I said. "They haven't closed school yet . . . or stopped public gatherings like they did in New England. And haven't you and Mother always told me to do the right thing? Helping sick people is the right thing. And helping our soldiers is the right thing. You and Mother and Gram are taking risks every day to help people. I think I should too. I want to help. We'll be outside. There won't be as many germs. Please, Daddy. Let us have the lemonade sale."

Dad scratched the back of his head. "What do your girlfriends' parents think?"

"Grace said her parents would do what you thought best. I don't know about Janet or Winnie."

"So, if I say yes and you all catch the flu, then I'm responsible."

"Daddy, it's for the war."

"Joe, the Board of Health hasn't closed anything down . . . " At least Mother sounded a little bit on my side.

"Yet." Dad finished her sentence. He took a deep breath and sighed. "If the Board of Health closes anything, there's no lemonade sale."

I hugged my father, "Thank you, Daddy!"

He hugged me extra tight. "I hope this is not a mistake."

CHAPTER THIRTEEN

FOUR-MINUTE GIRL

As soon as the paper arrived Saturday morning, I checked the headlines to see if the Board of Health had closed anything. The only mention of influenza was a report of a thousand new cases in the last twenty-four hours at Camp Dix. Seventy-four soldiers died from the flu in one day—a new record. *These numbers are so big. Can they be right?* Despite the risk, women were volunteering to help the sick soldiers. A quarantine notice would probably be on the front page, but I checked the whole paper just in case. Good! No closings. The lemonade sale was still on.

At Janet's house, we painted a sign: "Keep the Kaiser Away—Buy Lemonade Today. 10¢" When we were done, Grace and I got the lemons and made syrup with my grandmother. We were ready. Now if no one closed down public places in the next twenty-four hours, we were set.

Sunday morning, I was up early to check the news. Dad was too. He held up *The New York Times* so I could see the front page. "They're closing schools and public places in Boston," he said.

"But they're *not* in New York." I pointed to another article and held up the *Sunday Home News.* "There's nothing in the paper here, either. See?"

Dad grimaced, but I knew he'd keep his word.

Later that morning, Fred helped Winnie and Janet bring the lemonade stand down to the church lawn. Grace and I brought the cups and gallon jars of lemonade in the wagon. We thumbtacked our sign to the front of the stand. Then I remembered. We didn't have the cigar box with the change. I ran back to the store, but luckily, I met Gram halfway. She had the money, and I raced back with it to the church grounds. Fred thought he should test the lemonade for us. "Okay, but only one glass, and that's payment for helping us," Janet told her brother.

Churchgoers chatted on the lawn before heading home to Sunday dinners. A few men were our first customers. It wasn't long until some ladies brought their children for a drink. We kept pouring lemonade and making change. Children pestered their mothers for second helpings.

Then oddly, everyone stopped talking. I heard Mrs. Detwiler's voice complaining that it was wrong to sell things on a Sunday. The Sabbath was a day of rest. What was the world coming to? She strolled over to our lemonade stand. "Do your parents know what you are doing?" She looked straight at Gram and Mrs. Gardener. "And Pastor McElroy, did he approve?" Mrs. Detwiler played to the crowd. "There are laws in this state prohibiting commerce on Sundays."

My face grew hot with embarrassment. Suddenly I felt guilty. Were we breaking a law or worse, one of the Ten Commandments? The pastor had given us permission. Still, I felt ashamed and my chin trembled, but I forced myself not to cry. I had cried enough this year on account of the Detwilers.

I couldn't look at Mrs. Detwiler, so I stared at the drops of water that ran down the glass lemonade jug. I felt an ache in the pit of my stomach. I remembered how she had been so mean to the sweethearts at Van Drusen's. I *had* to stand up to Billy's mother. "We're raising money for the Liberty Loan."

"Josie, we can't hear what you're saying," she said sharply. "My Billy has been practicing Four-Minute speeches, and he can stand up and be heard just as well as any man."

By this time, Pastor McElroy had moved closer to the lemonade stand. "Billy. Why, yes. A dear boy. We haven't seen Billy in a while on Sundays."

Someone snickered.

123

Momentarily checked, Mrs. Detwiler stood with her mouth open.

Out of the blue, Grace said, "We want to squish the Kaiser."

There were a few chuckles, and I could see heads nodding in agreement.

Winnie was so close to me I could feel her shaking. She whispered, "What's your stupid son doing for the Liberty Loan?"

Mrs. Detwiler glared at us. "Did you say something, Josie?"

Winnie squeezed my hand. "Ohhh no," she said under her breath.

Mrs. Detwiler huffed and turned to walk away, but the crowd wouldn't move.

I looked for Gram, but instead I saw Miss Penny. I thought about her fiancé and the war bond flyer that told how Liberty Bonds could help soldiers.

"Mrs. Detwiler," I started in a tiny voice, "we will use this money to buy War Savings Stamps." My throat was so dry I wanted to guzzle down all the lemonade.

I looked at Miss Penny. She mouthed, "Loud-*er*."

I took a deep breath. "A War Savings Stamp will feed a soldier for a month. If we can buy five War Savings Books, we will give our government enough money to buy three hundred doses of typhoid serum or ether to make surgery painless for wounded soldiers. Or twenty-five dollars will buy bandages and crutches."

Silence. The crowd looked like the mannequins in store windows. Then a clap. And another clap. People applauded.

Pastor McElroy put a dime next to the pitcher. "My treat." He handed a cup of lemonade to Mrs. Detwiler.

She looked like she had just bitten into a lemon rind. Through pursed lips, she said, "Since it is for the Liberty Loan." She turned again, and this time the crowd let her through. She's going to hate me forever, I thought.

Suddenly everyone was buying more lemonade. Pastor McElroy told us his sermon should have been about the Lord and the Pharisees, and I saw Grace's mother give Gram the "Can you believe this?" look.

Miss Penny came through the crowd. "Oh Josie, that was wonderful! It may not have been four minutes, but it was mightily effective. You get an A." And she said to all of us, "You girls are all wonderful."

Gram hugged me. "It's too bad your parents are minding the store. They would have loved to hear your speech. They're going to be so proud." Under her breath, she said to Grace's mother, "And a little sorry they missed the fireworks."

After expenses, we made $8.30, or about two dollars each when split four ways. Two dollars was enough for me to buy eight Thrift Stamps to add to the eight I already had. Enough to buy another $5.00 War Savings Stamp and feed a soldier.

After dinner, I rehearsed the speech for school.

Partway through, Mother yawned. "Oh, excuse me," she said. "I didn't mean to yawn. It's not your speech. It's me." She shivered and pulled her sweater around her shoulders. "I'm a little tired tonight."

CHAPTER FOURTEEN

MY WORST FEAR

"Josie, I have to pee."

I awoke with a start. A little hand shook my shoulder.

"Where's Grandma? I need to go to the bathroom," Tiny whispered.

There was light under the bedroom door, and I heard voices in the kitchen. Gram must be up. But why?

The light hurt my eyes as I stepped into the hall. Squinting, I could just see Dad and Gram at the kitchen table. I turned on the bathroom light for Tiny.

"What time is it?" I asked.

"Two-thirty," said Gram.

Had Dad been out on another midnight call like when Tony's mother was sick?

"Joe." Mother called from the sitting room next to the kitchen. She sounded different. Sleepy-like. *Why is she in there?*

"Son, you need your own sleep," Gram said. "I'll take care of Ethel. You take care of yourself." She went into the sitting room.

"What's wrong?" I asked.

Dad motioned for me to come closer. He put his arm around my waist. "I think your mother may be coming down with the flu."

My stomach went into a knot. "Like Tony's mother?"

Dad hugged me. "Don't worry. She'll pull through."

Tiny padded into the kitchen. "Where's Momma?"

"Just peek in at the door. Don't go in," Dad said.

Mother was lying on the sofa, propped up by several pillows. Her arm was draped across her forehead, her face pinched and pained. In a small voice she said to Gram, "My head is pounding."

"The aspirin should work soon." Gram adjusted the wet washcloth on Mother's forehead, and Mother closed her eyes.

Tiny ran over to the sofa.

"Clementine." Mother shook her finger at my sister. "Don't come any closer. I don't want you to get sick."

Dad picked up my sister and carried her out to the kitchen.

"Girls," Mother said, closing her eyes again, "I'll see you in the morning."

Gram whispered, "Go to bed. We will need our strength. Let your mother sleep."

Tiny got in bed with me. It was hard to sleep because my worst fears about Spanish influenza were coming true. *Would Mother die? Like Mrs. Santorini?* I prayed and held my sister close.

∞

I dreamt Billy Detwiler was coughing. I woke up and realized Mother was coughing in the next room. Water was running in the bathroom as if someone was taking a bath. I slipped out of bed to see what was going on.

Dad was carrying Mother into the bathroom. Even though she was still in her nightgown, Dad put her right in the tub of water.

She yelped and started thrashing. "It's freezing! Get me out of here!" The words just jumped out of her.

"Easy. Your fever is 105 degrees," Dad said.

"Ohhh! It's like ice cubes!"

"You're burning up," Dad said. "The water's tepid. You just think it's cold because of your fever."

Gram brought an ice bag and tried to put it on Mother's head, but Mother wouldn't hold still.

Dad helped Mother lie down in the water. He held her with one arm and scooped water over Mother's head. "She's delirious."

They kept this up for I don't know how long: tepid water, ice, Mother not making any sense. I had never seen anyone in a fever delirium, let alone my mother.

The noise awakened Tiny. She came into the hall. She clutched my nightgown with one hand and with the other stuck her finger in her mouth.

"Josie, get a clean nightgown for your mother," Gram ordered.

I bolted up to my parents' third-floor bedroom, taking two steps at a time.

Dad pulled Mother up by her shoulders and Gram got Mother's feet. Mother still struggled. They managed to get her to sit on a towel on the commode. Gram pulled off Mother's sopping nightgown and draped towels around her to dry her off.

Gram dried Mother's arms and body. I grabbed a towel and rubbed Mother's feet and calves. Her teeth chattered, and she was shaking. I was shaking too. It was frightening to see her like this.

"Josie," Gram said. "There are clean sheets on the chair in the sitting room. Strip the sheets off the couch. They're drenched with sweat. Put clean ones on as best you can. Use the clean mattress pad too."

I rushed to smooth and tuck in the sheets.

When I got back to the bathroom, Gram said, "Fever's down — 103.5."

Mother shivered in her clean nightgown as Gram tried to dry her hair. Mother's eyes looked sunken and she had dark circles around her eye. "My head hurts so much. Please don't touch it," she said.

Dad carried Mother back to the couch. Gram tucked her in with the sheet. I put a dry towel on the pillow to absorb more water.

In the morning, coffee was on the stove and a used cup was in the sink. I peeked into the sitting room. No Dad. He must be in the store already. Mother was sleeping, and Gram was slumped in a chair, her feet on the ottoman and the afghan sliding off her. I pulled the afghan up to cover Gram. She snortled but didn't wake up. I made myself jelly bread for breakfast.

At school my fears about the speech and my money for the Liberty Loan disappeared into thin air. I couldn't help worrying about Mother.

When I got home for lunch, Mother was sleeping on the sofa with a cold compress on her forehead. Blankets were folded at her feet. Only a sheet tucked her in.

In the kitchen, more chicken soup cooled in Mason jars. Gram had made chicken soup every day since

Spanish influenza had come to town. Now the soup was for us. Gram was finishing the breakfast dishes. "How was the speech?" Gram asked.

"Fine. But hardly anyone was in school today to hear it," I said as I squished in next to Gram at the sink to wash my hands.

"Do any of your friends have flu yet?"

"Eight were absent today, but Grace, Winnie, and Janet were in school." I dried my hands. "The principal visited our class today. He was pretty cross because somebody's been vandalizing the bathrooms."

"Just what we need," Gram said as she scoured the soup pot. "Like we don't have enough trouble in the world — young people have to pull stupid stunts."

As I started my sandwich, I could hear Mother coughing. Suddenly I wasn't hungry.

At dinnertime Doc Fagan came up to see Mother again. Mother's temperature was still 103 degrees. She sounded like she had a head cold, her nose was so stuffy. And her cough was getting worse. And she was weak, so weak we had to help her take sips of water. But her biggest complaint was pain. Pain in her head. Pain all over her body. Aspirin alone was not working.

Dr. Fagan consulted Dad. "Phenacetin?"

"It takes a couple hours to really work," Dad said. "Phenocoll Hydrochloride is faster and shouldn't upset her stomach."

"We'll try the Phenocoll," the doctor said. "And we might think about switching to Brown Mixture if the cough gets worse."

Tiny and I watched from the doorway. Doc Fagan listened to Mother's chest with his stethoscope. With his hand, he thumped around her back and shoulders, listening for sounds that would tell him if Mother was developing pneumonia.

"All we can do is keep her comfortable," Doctor Fagan said once he was back in the kitchen. "The next few days will tell."

CHAPTER FIFTEEN

SCHOOL CLOSES

I didn't sleep much last night because of Mother's coughing. Gram wasn't sleeping either. I could hear her in the kitchen chipping ice for Mother. How long would it be before Gram came down with the flu too?

At breakfast time, Tiny and Gram were still sleeping soundly. Mother was too. Dad and I tiptoed around the kitchen. He made coffee, and I made oatmeal. If Gram were in the kitchen with me, she'd tell me to watch the oatmeal like a hawk so it wouldn't burn. It was unpatriotic to waste food, she'd say. I kept stirring and stirring so it wouldn't stick to the pan.

When Dad checked on Mother, I watched from the doorway. He felt her cheeks and forehead for fever, but he didn't wake her. He held her wrist and took her pulse. As he came back into the kitchen he whispered, "She's still feverish." He poured a fresh glass of ice water for Mother and left it on the table next to the sofa. "Josie," he said softly, "stay home until your grandmother gets up. You can go to school late."

School was so important to my father. I was surprised he suggested I should stay home.

"Let everybody sleep as long as they can," he said as he wrote a note. "Give this to Miss Penny when you get to school. And if your Mother has trouble, come get me."

At first I didn't know what to do. I decided to wash our dishes, trying to use hot-hot water like Gram did. After that I watched Mother sleeping. *How long does flu last?* Maybe the worst was over and she would improve. I hoped, and I said another prayer.

Gram stretched and yawned as she came into the kitchen. "Why are you still here?"

"Daddy wanted me to stay until you got up. There's oatmeal and coffee on the stove." I felt proud of myself. "I hope it's all right."

Brrring.

We jumped at the sound of the telephone. Dad had an extra bell ringer installed in our apartment so he could hear the store telephone day or night.

"I hope that doesn't wake your mother," Gram said.

I peeked at Mother on the couch. She was fast asleep.

"You can go to school now, Josie," Gram said.

As I got my sweater and book bag, I heard Dad. He had come back up from the store.

"That was Principal Springfield." Dad kept his voice low. "He called to tell me he talked to Fagan. They decided to close the school at noon. Josie, you might as well stay home this morning. Four teachers and over two hundred students are absent. Fagan wants me to send over fumigators."

"When will school reopen?" I asked.

"Thursday. We need a day or so for the gas to kill germs, and then we need to air out the building.

"Maybe this is a good thing," Gram said. "With Ethel down with the flu, we can use the help."

Help meant doing dishes and laundry and sweeping the kitchen floor with a wet broom to keep dust and germs from floating into the air. Today we washed sheets and towels. Tiny helped scrub towels on the metal washboard in the laundry tub. When it came time to rinse, boil, and add bluing to the water, we had to keep Tiny away. Bluing made the sheets look whiter, but it could stain your skin. And boiling water? We wanted to kill germs, not ourselves, so we all had to be careful. Since the sheets and towels were too hot to handle, we turned our attention to Mother. Gram took Mother's temperature. She still ran a fever.

"How do you feel?" Gram asked, holding Mother's wrist.

"Awful. The headache's coming back," Mother said. Then she coughed for what seemed like a half-hour.

"Can you sit up enough to take a pill?" Gram asked.

Mother tried to sit up by herself, and Gram moved the pillows to give her support. When Gram gave Mother the tablet, Mother couldn't swallow it. She started to cough and choke. She spit the pill out into her hand. "Crush it," she said as she kept coughing.

"Bring me two spoons, Josie," Gram said. "And some orange juice, please."

Gram crushed the tablet in between the two spoons until it was a powder. Then she mixed orange juice into the crushed medicine. That's what Mother and Gram had done for me before I could swallow pills. I knew the juice would taste good and go down easily.

We gave Mother tea and a little bit of oatmeal that was thinned out with water until it looked like soup. Mother was so weak that Gram had to feed her little spoonfuls as if she were a baby.

Later the laundry was cool enough to handle. "Tiny, you stay away from this wringer," Gram cautioned. We used a mechanical wringer, the kind with double rollers and a crank. You had to be careful feeding laundry in between the rollers while they were moving, because if you got your fingers caught, they would be crushed.

How did my mother and grandmother do this every day and pay attention so they didn't injure themselves, all while Tiny was following them around asking questions and wanting to help?

After lunch Tiny and I went downstairs to help Dad in the store. Tiny's banishment was over. She brought her shoebox filled with paper dolls and the clothes we had cut from magazines. I hoped they would keep her occupied.

Since school was out, a steady trickle of kids came in the store for penny candy and ice cream. It seemed like every two minutes I had to stop and wait on kids who had nothing to do on a rainy afternoon. Normally lots of business at the soda fountain was a good thing, but today it was a nuisance. Dad grumbled that one of the reasons to close school was to keep children away from each other so they wouldn't spread flu. Finally Dad decided to close the soda fountain and penny candy counter.

Shortly afterward, Billy Detwiler and two boys came in the store. Were they the same two boys I saw outside of Van Drusens's Pharmacy? Billy pointed at my sister and then to the register in the back. "Watch out for *Phlegm*entine," he said. They laughed.

Looking up over her dolls, my sister gave Billy a dark scowl. "My name's Clementine!"

They laughed again and sat down at the counter. "We'll have phosphates," Billy said.

"Fountain's closed," I declared.

Billy leered at me. "What's the matter, Pharmacy Girl? Can't your slacker father keep up with the business?" The other boys laughed and made barking noises.

The hair on my back rose. Luckily, just then Mr. Oliver, the school custodian, came in the store. He gave Billy and his friends a cold stare.

The boys slid off the stools faster than eels slip through water. "Let's get out of here and go to New Brunswick where they have better ice cream."

"I'm here to pick up the fumigators," the custodian said to Dad. "Sorry I couldn't get over sooner. Those darn kids are still causing trouble. Yesterday it was toilet paper all over the boys' lavatory. Today, one of the little hooligans stuffed a roll of toilet paper in a commode and caused a minor flood. We didn't have this problem last year. Three guesses who the prime suspect is. No wonder he got kicked out of prep school."

Dad raised his eyebrows.

Mr. Oliver pointed his thumb towards the door. "And if he's hanging around those Mackenzie boys, it won't be long until the Detwiler boy is on to more than vandalism."

"You know those boys?" Dad asked.

"The Mackenzies live next to my sister in New Brunswick. She's always telling me about their stunts."

Dad put a large box on the counter. "There are enough fumigators for each classroom, the hallways, bathrooms, and the office."

"Don't worry, Doc." Mr. Oliver was optimistic. "These fumigators will knock out this flu just like Pershing's knocking out those Germans."

CHAPTER SIXTEEN

QUARANTINE

I'm so tired of oatmeal, I thought as I ate breakfast. *Toast. Cinnamon toast with a pound of butter and a sack of sugar would taste so good right now.*

Every day seemed the same: Care for Mother. Do laundry. Help Dad in the store. Watch Tiny.

About ten o'clock, Doctor Fagan came to see Mother. He said she would need to stay in bed until her temperature was normal, and we would have to be careful not to let her exert herself and run the risk of developing pneumonia. "Good food, palliatives, tender loving care — that's what she needs."

"Mother looks so helpless lying on the couch," I said to Gram.

"Stay busy. It will keep your mind from worrying too much," she said.

Gram sent me to Gephardt's for eggs and milk. She let me iron pillowcases and handkerchiefs. She showed me how to make Jell-O. I delivered prescriptions on my scooter. I still wore a surgical mask to protect me from germs, and I still had to leave the deliveries on the doorsteps of houses where there was flu. As I scooted over to Fourth Avenue I thought, *I live in a house where there is flu. If I'm going to catch it, I'll catch it right at home.*

Now I was allowed to go into the sitting room with Mother. Gram and I gave her a sponge bath and put her into a clean nightgown. She wanted to try sitting up in the chair. I tucked a blanket across her legs. Then I straightened the sheets on the couch and plumped the pillows.

"What day is it?" Mother asked.

"Friday," I said.

"Friday? How long have I been sleeping here?"

"Since Sunday night," Gram said.

"Good heavens! That long?" Mother touched the long braid that hung over her shoulder. "Friday." She started to unbraid her hair, then stopped. "Why aren't you in school?"

"School is closed on account of flu," I explained. "We've been home since Tuesday."

Mother tried to comb her hair with her fingers. "Can you get my comb and brush, please, Josie?"

I offered to brush Mother's hair. She leaned back against the cushioned upholstery. Gently I pulled her hair up and over the top of the chair. I started brushing the

144

ends to get knots out without pulling too much. It took a while since no one had brushed Mother's hair in days. Finally I was able to run both the brush and the comb all the way from the roots to the tips.

"That feels so relaxing," Mother said, coughing a little. "I might fall back asleep."

"Think you can stay awake long enough for something to eat? It's almost lunchtime," Gram said.

But Mother fell asleep as I braided her hair.

After lunch Gram went to the bank, Mother napped, and I kept Tiny occupied. Luckily, Tiny loved dressing paper dolls, so that helped to pass the time. But after a while, she wanted me to bake cookies so we could have a tea party for the dolls. I said no, we could not do that. We needed to conserve sugar, flour, and butter for soldiers and starving people in France. Then she wanted to go outside and ride in the toy car. If I sat in one of the rocking chairs on the back porch, I could watch Tiny outside while keeping an ear out for Mother in case she needed me.

As I rocked, I looked at my hands on my lap. They felt rough and sore. It must be all the washing—dishes, laundry, germs off my hands.

"Jooo-seee, can I go out front?" my sister whined from the yard. "It's too hard to drive on the grass."

"No, stay back here so I can watch you and listen for Mother."

I started rocking again. When had I last seen my friends? Was it only a week ago that we were planning our lemonade sale? What was Grace doing? Janet and Winnie? Did their families have flu yet? I wished I could visit or they could come over. For now, we were all stuck at home. Well, at least I was.

Tiny called to me from the bottom of the stairs. She wanted ice cream.

I checked on Mother. She wanted some ice cream too. Since her fever was down, she could have milk without it upsetting her stomach.

When Tiny and I stepped into the pharmacy, I saw that tea towels were now covering the glasses lining the back shelves of the soda fountain. Dad was serious about keeping the fountain closed.

"Use the take-home cartons," Dad said. "And take some syrup with you too. In a few days we'll only have to throw it out."

As I dished ice cream into the waxed cardboard containers, Doctor Fagan arrived.

"Hello, ladies." Doc Fagan tipped his hat at Tiny and me. "Getting your last treats in before Monday?"

"What do you mean, Dr. Fagan?" I asked.

"Did you hear?" the doctor asked Dad. "The County Board of Health is closing public places. New

Brunswick closed schools today, and theaters, restaurants, and soda fountains will be closed Monday until further notice. How's Ethel?"

"The girls are taking her ice cream. She slept better last night," Dad said.

"Good. I'll still go up to see her."

"Tell me more about the closing order," Dad asked.

As I put strawberry syrup in a container, I kept my ears wide open.

"I ask you, how is waiting until Monday going to help limit the spread of flu? At least you're ahead of the game, closing the fountain already," Doc said. "And I hate to say I told you so, but the Liberty Loan rallies are not affected by the order."

"I want sprinkles," Tiny interrupted.

I put my finger to my lips to tell Tiny to be quiet. I put chocolate sprinkles in another container.

"Of course, public officials don't want to cause any alarm." The doctor sounded annoyed. "Officials are saying, 'Don't panic.' They're only taking this new measure because the flu could interfere with war work." The doctor ran his finger around the inside of his high collar. "For God's sake, doctors all over the county are having a devil of a time keeping up with new cases, and the death rate—it's unheard of! But let's not panic."

"Don't let anyone hear you complaining like that," Dad warned. "All we need in the middle of an epidemic is to have the town's only doctor dragged off to jail for sedition."

It was a good thing Mrs. Detwiler wasn't around. She'd report the doctor for what he said, and then she'd report Dad and me for listening. She probably would report Tiny just for spite.

"Just blowing off steam." With his hands on his hips, he stretched his head and neck backwards.

"How long will the epidemic last?" I asked.

The doctor finished stretching. "Influenza outbreaks typically run four to six weeks—of course, Spanish influenza is a long way from typical." He paused. "If it started here mid-September, it could be Halloween before we are out of the woods."

"God help us," my father said.

That scared me. I closed the ice cream containers, and we headed back upstairs.

"Ah, the fair nurses bearing delectable sustenance to the sick," Doctor Fagan teased. "I hope there's enough for me." And as we left the store, he said, "And Joe, you look like h---."

Yes, he said that word.

"Get some sleep, man. You're working too hard."

"Look who's talking," Dad laughed.

But I worried. Was Dad working too hard? Was his resistance down? Would it be easier for him to catch the flu?

CHAPTER SEVENTEEN

EXPLOSION!

Mother had improved enough to sit with us at dinner. She even giggled a bit as she watched Tiny help with the dishes. Tiny was whipping up soapsuds with the eggbeater when our neighbor, Mrs. Senker, popped in with bread pudding for Mother. The fragrance of freshly made custard and cinnamon filled the kitchen. Everybody had a taste.

"Do you think Daddy would like some?" I asked.

"I bet he would," said Mother.

I scooped a dish of pudding for him and took it down to the store.

The sun was far enough down now that we needed the electric lights. The store was quiet, the electric fans motionless overhead.

"Daddy, I brought you some bread pudding."

Dad sat down in the store's wheelchair and propped his feet up. "It smells delicious." While he ate the dessert, I pulled a chair next to him. We watched the sunlight slant lower through the front windows, making everything pinkish and golden. The regulator clock ticked and chimed the half hour.

"Josie, I'm very proud of all the things you've been doing to help your mother and Gram and me," Dad said.

I tucked my feet up on the chair and hugged my knees. I loved being in the store with him. "Daddy, I'm glad I can help."

He finished the pudding, scraping the bottom of the bowl as if he were a little kid getting the last bit. "We should do something patriotic with the store windows for the Liberty Loan," Dad said. "Something more than just the bond posters. Let's do something fancy like they're doing in New Brunswick. What do you think?"

"That's a great—" A low booming sound interrupted my sentence. Glassware in the store tinkled with the vibration. *Thunder?*

My father heard it too. He sat up in the chair, alert. We listened. The rumbling continued. There was another boom, followed by several more. The globes on the lights rattled along with the glassware.

"That's not firecrackers, is it?" I said.

Dad was out of the chair now, and I followed him out front to the street. He looked west toward New Brunswick. He turned and looked east toward Woodbridge. The booming continued.

Neighbors poured onto Raritan Avenue. Everyone wondered what was going on. Grace's family joined us.

"George thinks it's fireworks," Grace said.

"Or shells exploding," said Frank.

We stood there in a little cluster, listening to adults wondering which munitions factory was in trouble.

"Maybe German submarines are off Sandy Hook shelling New York City," George said.

Now I was getting a little scared. The explosions continued to reverberate down Raritan Avenue toward the river.

"I think Frank Junior's right," Dad said. "It sounds like shells blowing up — and a lot of them. It might be the Gillespie Plant."

The Gillespie Munitions Works. I whispered to Grace. "Gillespie is the biggest ammunition loading plant in the world."

"Joe! Gardener!" Chief McMurtry ran over to the store from the firehouse. "I just got the call! Major explosion at Gillespie!" The chief caught his breath. "It knocked out windows in South Amboy. We're sending the truck. Half our men are flat on their backs with flu. We need everyone we can get." Frank and George wanted to go, but the chief wanted them to take messages at the station. Grace's father and brothers ran with the chief for the firehouse.

153

"Come on, Josie!" As we ran into the store, Dad said, "Grab all the bandages and adhesive tape." He dumped the boxes holding the Red Cross linens on the floor. "Put things in here." I could hear the fire bell clanging. Next Dad pulled first aid kits off the shelves and threw them into the box. "We need the sterile cotton. All of it."

An automobile horn honked. Doctor Fagan left the motor running and dashed into the store shouting, "Gillespie's blowing up!"

"I know!" Dad hollered from the back of the store.

I pointed to the box of bandages. Dad gathered morphine and syringes. Doc Fagan found the antiseptics and stuffed them into his pockets. Then he hurried to put the box of supplies into his car.

"Grab those rubber gloves, Josie," the doctor ordered.

We ran out of the store. Doc Fagan and Dad jumped into the car. I threw the gloves on top of the bandages in the back seat.

"Hold down the fort, Josie!" Dad handed me the pharmacy keys. "Lock up and say a prayer no one here needs us tonight." The car sped away, honking all the while and Dad waving madly as they passed the firehouse to let the chief know he was with the doctor.

Gram met me in the store. We locked up the poisons and the controlled drugs. Gram tidied the shelves where we had grabbed supplies. I refolded and stacked the Red Cross linens in the window. It was dark now, and still the explosions continued. We checked the stamps and the revolver, emptied the cash drawers, put the money in the safe, switched off the lights, and locked the doors. I hoped the Labor Day thief would not think to rob the store tonight.

At bedtime I prayed for the Gillespie workers and all the people helping. I prayed no one in Highland Park would need a prescription, a doctor, or a fireman.

CHAPTER EIGHTEEN

GILLESPIE

I woke up to the dull, thudding sounds of explosions, which must have been why I'd been dreaming about Billy Detwiler riding his bicycle on Raritan Avenue, dropping giant cherry bombs as he flew along. In my dream I'd shouted at him, "Stop it! Stop it! The windows are breaking!" And then he'd turned into the Kaiser and laughed like an evil fiend.

An automobile's engine cut off in front of the store. Car doors creaked open and banged shut. I peeked out the window. It was Dad and Mr. Gebhart. I hurried into the kitchen.

"Just in time, Josie," said Gram. "Do you want your eggs scrambled or sunny-side-up?"

"Daddy's home," I said as he came through the door.

Dad smelled like smoke, and he had dirt and soot on his face and clothes. But Mother still hugged him. "You all have to go outside," Dad said.

"What?" we said.

"The seven-day magazines could blow up. An explosion that big could make our house collapse."

Mother gaped at him.

Another explosion boomed in the distance.

"Ethel! Listen to me." Dad grabbed Mother by her shoulders. "Glass storefronts in New Brunswick are shattering from the explosions." He spoke slowly as if he were talking to Tiny. "Get dressed. You need to go outside." He looked around at Tiny and me. "*All* of you."

"Are you going back?" Mother asked.

"Yes. Gebhart came with me to take injured workers to the hospital. He's at his store getting food for the Red Cross." Dad ran his fingers through his hair. "Fagan and Gardener are still at the plant. People in South Amboy have been out in the streets all night for fear their houses could collapse."

"If the next explosion could knock down our house, then what will happen to you if you're right there next to the plant!" Mother exclaimed.

"These people need all the help they can get." Dad shooed me toward the bedroom. "What are you waiting for? Get your clothes on."

By the time we were dressed, Gram had made our eggs into sandwiches and wrapped them up for Dad. "You want coffee?" she asked.

"No. The Red Cross is out in full force and there's plenty of coffee everywhere." Dad stuffed the sandwiches in his coat pockets. "I don't know when I'll be home." He kissed Mother and ruffled my hair. Tiny's too. "Keep the windows open," he said, and as fast as he had appeared, he was gone.

"All right, you three," Gram said. "Outside. It doesn't take long to fry eggs. I'll bring breakfast down. Josie, get sweaters and blankets."

Ten minutes later we were all outside. Gram and I carried the store's wheelchair to the middle of the backyard for Mother.

As I started my egg sandwich, Grace came running across the back yards. "Is it true? Could an explosion knock buildings down?" But before I could answer, Grace made a disgusted face.

I turned around and there was Billy Detwiler in our alley on his bicycle.

"How come the store's closed?" he sneered. "Your slacker father sleeping late?"

"My father is at Gillespie helping the injured, in case you hadn't heard."

"Do you think I'm deaf? Besides, your slacker father is good for nothing!" Billy called as he rode away.

I stomped my foot. He made my blood boil!

Around ten o'clock we heard an enormous explosion—the biggest we'd heard so far. It made me duck and cover my ears. Tiny started crying and climbed on Mother's lap. Grace and I went out front to check the store windows. No broken glass. Explosions, although not the big one we were expecting, continued all morning, but no buildings came down in Highland Park.

After lunch, Dad called. The danger from the seven-day magazines had passed. But he couldn't talk long because telephone operators were swamped with emergency calls. He still didn't know when he'd be home.

"Thank goodness we can go inside," Gram said. "With nighttime temperatures in the forties and influenza around every corner, nobody should sleep in the open, especially you, Ethel."

The exertion of going upstairs was too much for Mother. She immediately slumped onto the sofa and started coughing. There was barely enough cough syrup left in the bottle to dot the spoon. I knew where we kept the Brown Mixture in the store. "I'll be back in a jiffy, Mother," I said.

Mother rolled her eyes. "'Jiffy.' Such slang, Josie."

I hunted my brain for a good, grown-up word. "I will be back *directly*."

Mother gently shook her head and smiled. "You are quite the character!"

Once we got Mother settled, I still had papers to deliver.

As I went from house to house, I read snippets from the front page. Hundreds of doctors, nurses, and volunteer firemen were at Gillespie, but soldiers kept them away from the fire and the danger of more explosions. Ambulances carried wounded to hospitals as far away as Northern New Jersey and New York. Perth Amboy was under martial law, and soldiers were sent to prevent looting. The explosions damaged two churches in South Amboy. The stained-glass windows of St. Mary's were shattered, and the roof of Sacred Heart had been blown off. It made me think of the Liberty Loan poster of the burning church, and it made my skin crawl.

~

By seven o'clock, Dad was still not home. Tiny was getting a bath. Mother and Tiny sang "This is the way we scrub our backs . . . " while Gram washed Tiny's back with a soapy washcloth. Mother sat on the side of the tub with a towel. This was so much better than the time I saw Mother in the tub delirious with fever. Singing made Mother cough. Once Tiny was in bed, Mother tried to read aloud to her, but bath time had sapped all her strength. I read *Raggedy Ann* to Tiny.

Later in the sitting room, I asked Mother if she had seen the article in the paper about the telephone operator. "It said she was a half mile from the explosions, and she had stayed on duty calling all over the county for help despite the danger. Do you think she was the one who called Doctor Fagan and Chief McMurtry?" I wanted to be brave like that.

"Possibly." Mother yawned and put the latest *McCall's* on the coffee table. "Do you want to look at the magazine?"

"No, thank you." I didn't feel like reading.

"Don't you have some socks you were working on for the soldiers?"

I didn't feel like knitting either.

"Try not to worry, Josie." Mother sank back into her pillows. "Why don't you make us some chamomile tea? Lots of honey and lemon, please."

As I put the kettle on to boil, Gram had finished her bath and came into the kitchen. She looked around. "No sign of your father?"

I wondered how worried she was.

By the time the tea was ready, Mother was sound asleep. Gram felt Mother's forehead and settled into a chair with the magazine Mother had offered me earlier. I left Mother's tea on the table and tucked her in. The clock chimed nine. I turned out the electric light closest to Mother, got comfortable in the other armchair, and pulled the afghan over myself. As I sipped my tea, I could hear the clock ticking in the kitchen. What if Dad never came home? I looked at Gram. She smiled at me and turned a page.

Both my grandfathers died before I was born. Grandfather Winslow died from a burst appendix at thirty-five, roughly Dad's age now. My mother's father also died in his mid-thirties, but I didn't know why. Neither of my grandmothers remarried, and they each had three children to raise alone. Somehow they managed. We could do that. But what if Mother . . .

Then I thought, *Stop! Stop! Don't think that way! I can hope. And pray.* Mother seemed to be getting better. Hope and prayer had worked. I said another little prayer, just in case.

‰

By Sunday afternoon Dad was still not home. Saturday's store chores still needed doing. I dusted, swept, and polished glass. Then we counted inventory. Gram sat in the wheelchair with the ledger book in her lap as I counted stock. "We'll need more bandages and adhesive tape when the Johnson & Johnson man comes on Tuesday," I said.

"We'll need Synol, too," Gram said, jotting it down.

"Do you think we'll go to the Liberty Loan parade tomorrow?"

She kept writing in the inventory book. "I doubt it."

"Will people think we're unpatriotic if we don't go?"

"They shouldn't." Gram banged the pencil down on the ledger. "Who goes over to the Red Cross once a week with a donation? Who sells Liberty Bonds? Who practically gave away American flags last Memorial Day? Who's had a flag waving outside his store since the war began? Who's been up all hours of the night with this cursed flu! Who's over at the Gillespie Plant right now, risking his own life?" She shook her finger at me. "Your father, that's *who!* I'd like to see the person who thinks we're not patriotic!"

Wooooo! Gram usually didn't get riled up like this. What could I do? Change the subject? "Daddy wanted to decorate the store," I said. "For the Liberty Loan."

Gram put the inventory book away and sat back down in the wheelchair. She closed her eyes but kept talking. "We could use the bunting we used last time. It's on the shelf under the Kodaks."

The cameras were at the front of the store. I peeked out the window, hoping to see my father or at least Doctor Fagan's Maxwell coming down Raritan Avenue. Dad had never been away two nights, at least that I could remember.

"A watched pot never boils," Gram said, adjusting the footrest on the wheelchair.

I found red, white, and blue bunting and a box of small American flags. "Do you think I can use these little flags in the windows?"

"Why not? When it's time to hang the bunting, I'll help."

For the first time in weeks, I was doing something fun. *No one would think the Winslows were slackers!* "Gram, what do you think about a sign on the door? 'Buy Bonds Here.'" She snored softly in the wheelchair. Trying to be quiet, I arranged the flags in the front windows. Then I got poster board and drew letters for the sign. I made up red and blue poster paint in little jars. Shaking the jar to mix the red powder and the water, I wondered what old Mrs. Detwiler was doing for the Liberty Loan. *That old toad! I dare her to say we're not patriotic.*

Later on, in the midst of dinner, we heard footsteps on the stairs.

"Daddy!"

"Any food left for a hungry fireman?" he joked, coming through the door.

I jumped out of my chair to hug him. His face was whiskery, and he still smelled like smoke, but I didn't care.

Dad hugged us all, and Mother made him a plate of food while he washed up at the kitchen sink. "So, Joe, tell us the details," Mother said.

"Officials were worried that German agents might try to get in the plant. The soldiers made a deadline around the whole area."

"What's a deadline?" I asked.

"Soldiers had orders to shoot anyone who tried to cross it."

"Our soldiers would shoot our own people?" I found that hard to believe.

"They meant business," Dad said.

"Do they think it was sabotage?" I cleared my dishes.

Dad shrugged. "Don't know yet."

"It was cold last night. What about the people forced out of their houses?" Mother asked.

"The Red Cross handed out blankets and hot food to anyone who needed it."

"And what about you and Doctor Fagan?" Gram poured Dad hot coffee.

"We spent most of our time at the first aid station near the plant." He yawned. "Soldiers and sailors did the bulk of the rescue work. After the explosions stopped, they let volunteers help."

Dad sipped his coffee. "Every time there was an explosion all sorts of debris fell—shards of glass, hunks of wood, concrete, metal shell fragments. It made me think about what it must be like in the trenches."

"Did any workers get out?" I asked.

Dad nodded. "A good many climbed over the barbed-wire fence surrounding the plant, and then they crawled through the marsh to safety. Many of those men—injured themselves—carried other victims out of danger."

"What about the big explosion?" I asked. "The one you warned us about?"

"We were lucky there too. The fire did not get to the main TNT storage area, so the storage magazines were spared." Dad looked at Mother. "If we thought the explosions we experienced Friday and Saturday were bad—"

Mother interrupted, "You could have been injured or killed." Mother put her hand on Dad's arm.

He gave Mother a kiss on the forehead. "I know."

For the first time in a week, Mother decided she would sleep in her own bed. It was the first normal go-to-bed night in what seemed like a month—only it had just been a week of our lives being topsy-turvy.

CHAPTER NINETEEN

BACK PERSHING'S MEN: BUY BONDS AGAIN

On Monday I helped Dad catch up on weekend work. We bottled a batch of citrate of magnesia. People had been buying a lot lately because they thought cleaning out your system would help ward off diseases like influenza. We put lemon flavor in the laxative to make it taste better, but it was still nasty, especially since I knew what it was going to do. As I finished putting corks in the tops of the bottles, Mr. Horowitz, the baker, arrived.

"I just came back from delivering bread to the Red Cross for the people in South Amboy," declared the baker through his gauze mask, "and now, I am here to buy a Liberty Bond. I *vant* to be first."

Mr. Horowitz was a very nice man, but sometimes I had trouble understanding him because of his Austrian accent.

"You were my first bond customer last time," Dad said as he went to the safe.

Mr. Horowitz asked if Dad was home from the Gillespie Plant in time to go to the rally yesterday.

"I was sorry to miss the rally," Dad said, rubbing his knees as he got up from closing the safe.

"Such a terrible thing, Gillespie," Mr. Horowitz said. "Like the *var*. Like the explosion at Black Tom Island last year. This time, so many more are dead."

Mr. Horowitz gave Dad money for the War Bond.

"How was the Liberty Loan rally?" Dad asked, filling out the paperwork.

The baker's demeanor changed, his eyes glistened, and he gladly gave us all the details.

I gave Mr. Horowitz a Liberty Loan poster for his window and a pin.

"Wery nice," Mr. Horowitz said, pinning the button on his lapel. He polished the pin with his sleeve. "Thank you, Doc, and thank you, Josie." He gave us a courtly bow and whistled "Yankee Doodle" as he walked out onto the street.

"Why does Mr. Horowitz think the poster and the pin are so important?"

"So people know he bought a Liberty Bond. Some people get carried away with their patriotism and pressure folks to buy more bonds," Dad said. "They mean well, but they go too far. And other people don't like Germans or Austrians no matter how nice or how loyal they are to our country."

"Like Mr. Horowitz?"

Dad nodded. "Do you remember when his store was vandalized?"

"Do you mean last year, when someone painted 'slacker' on his store window and broke into the bakery?"

"It could have been thugs wanting to sell sugar and flour on the black market," Dad said. "But Samuel and Rose were convinced it was because they were Austrians and people thought they hadn't contributed enough to the Liberty Loan."

"But how would someone know how many bonds Mr. Horowitz bought?"

"We know who has bought bonds and how much they've spent. We just don't discuss it with anyone." Dad put the Bond Ledger in the stamp drawer.

"But how do *other* people know?" I asked again.

"Think about Fred and Tony. As Boy Scouts, they are asking for pledges from people to buy War Savings Stamps. People fill out cards that the Scouts give to the post office. They would know. Remember last year, when your class sold Thrift Stamps? You knew how much people bought. When women canvas their neighborhoods for the Liberty Loan, they know who promised to buy bonds and the amount. And sometimes

171

that information gets into the hands of people who go too far, like Mrs. Detwiler and the club she belongs to, the American Protective League. If she and her cronies think you haven't contributed enough, you're labeled unpatriotic. They'll call you a slacker, or a spy, or worst yet, a traitor."

"It's not right that someone as nice as Mr. Horowitz gets picked on and people like Mrs. Detwiler don't."

"Maybe it's because she's so prickly. Folks are a bit afraid of Gretchen."

"Are you afraid of her?"

Dad laughed. "Let's just put it this way. I'm wary. You don't see me poking sticks into hornets' nests, do you?"

"Do you think Mrs. Detwiler will say we're disloyal because we didn't go to the rally yesterday?"

"Let's hope she didn't notice," Dad said.

We heard a noise from the front of the store. "We'll be right with you," Dad called out.

"I wonder why we didn't hear the bell?" I asked.

Dad shrugged. "Preoccupied, I guess." He spun the dial on the lock. "See who that is, Josie, will you please?" Dad got up slowly from crouching at the safe.

I checked the mirror. Three boys. Billy Detwiler was leaning over the post office counter.

"It's Billy and those two boys." I remembered them from the day school closed.

Billy flinched and knocked over the Liberty Loan sign propped up on the glass. The two boys with Billy elbowed each other and smirked.

Dad came around the partition. "Hello, Billy. How can we help you today? The fountain's still closed, you know."

"Uh. Uh." Billy reached in his pocket. "My, my, mother needs some stamps." He looked at his change. "Just three."

"Your mother usually comes in for stamps," Dad said to Billy. "Is she all right? She doesn't have the flu, does she?"

"Oh no, she's fine," Billy said.

As the trio left, the bigger boy punched Billy in the arm. "Three *stamps?*"

❧

Later in the afternoon, Grace's father came in the store.

"More Liberty Loan supplies," Mr. Gardener called to Dad, "and I have a helper."

Grace popped out from behind her father. She carried a smaller package. Grace put her package down, and we both started dancing around.

"No hugging," Dad reminded. "We're just getting over flu here. Why don't you two chat outside in the fresh air?"

Grace and I sat on the back steps.

"Are you going to the parade tonight?" she asked.

"Probably not, because of the flu."

"My dad will go no matter what," Grace said. "He's a co-captain for the Liberty Loan. He told Mother it wouldn't look right if he didn't go to the kick-off parade."

The idea nagged me. Would people criticize my father if we weren't at the parade?

Grace kept talking. "I wish we could be in the parade. That was so much fun at Labor Day." She hugged her knees and looked glum. "I wish you could go with me."

I tucked my knees up under my chin. "Me too."

"What if we wore those masks?" Grace brightened. "Ask."

We went inside, but Dad only said, "We'll see. Frank, it might not be a bad idea for you to wear one." Dad put a half-dozen soft, white cotton surgical masks in a bag for Mr. Gardener.

Grace crossed her fingers as she left with her father, but I figured I was going to miss the parade.

≈

In the morning, Grace delivered more Liberty Loan materials to Dad.

"Did you go to the parade?" I asked.

"My parents wouldn't let us go, but . . . " Grace gave me a funny look. "Let's sit outside."

We sat on the step in front of the store. What was Grace up to?

"We went. Frank and George snuck over to the parade, and I went too," Grace whispered, checking over her shoulder to make sure no one was listening.

I clapped my hands over my mouth. "No. You didn't! Do your parents know?"

She shook her head. "They were at the reviewing stand up Albany Street, and we stayed near the bridge. But I hate to think what they will do if they find out. Oh Josie, I wish you could have been there! They had gigantic electric lights set up to illuminate the parade. It was bright as daylight. Frank said the lights were the same kind the army uses to light up battlefields."

"And he's right." My father stood in the doorway. "So, Grace, how was the parade?" Dad asked.

My eyes widened at Grace. Did he know?

"Weren't your father and mother at the parade?" Dad asked.

"Oh! They said the parade was great. You know, over the top."

"Good. I'm glad to hear it." Dad said, "What else did they say?"

Grace thought for a moment. "Wright-Martin had the best float. They had an aeroplane motor and girl workers showing how they build the engines. But the funny part was a few men from the plant dressed up in women's clothing to look like Liberty Girls. That was a good stunt. I mean, my father thought it was funny."

Dad nodded. "I bet it was."

A car slowed to a stop in front of the store. I recognized the Johnson & Johnson salesman getting out.

"Good morning, Joe," he said as he pulled a white surgical mask over his face. He tipped his hat and added, "Ladies."

We stood up so he could get by. He wore a Liberty Loan button on his lapel.

"I'm glad you're here," Dad said as he pushed open the screen door. "I used every bit of gauze and first aid supplies at the Gillespie explosion."

"We can fix that." The salesman stepped inside.

Grace filled me in on the rest of the parade. "And guess who saw us? Mrs. Detwiler. She asked me where my twin was, meaning you, and said she thought she would see all the Winslows right up front watching the parade."

She knows we didn't go. Horsefeathers!

Dad and the salesman came to the front door. "You heard the State Board of Health has closed churches," the Johnson and Johnson man said.

"That tells you how serious things are, doesn't it?" Dad held the door open again.

The salesman opened the trunk of his automobile and handed boxes of sterile gauze and cotton to Dad. Grace and I helped carry other supplies inside. Dad asked me to restock the shelves while he finished paperwork.

"May I help, Mr. Winslow?" Grace asked.

"Of course," Dad replied. "Do you know where the disinfectant soap goes?"

"Sure, Mr. Winslow. Would you like me to dust the shelf before I put the Synol bottles away?"

"Thank you, Grace," Dad said.

I had the feeling Grace was trying to make up for not really telling the truth to my father.

On Wednesday Mother dressed in regular clothes for the first time in over a week. She pulled the waist of her skirt out to show the gap. "I've lost weight." She got a safety pin and made a temporary alteration.

"Josie, can you please take the trash out? And take these newspapers too." She handed me a stack.

As I went down to the garbage, I couldn't help reading the articles. The Gillespie explosion looked like battlefields in Belgium and France. I read on. Smoke everywhere and shells exploding. It said the horses they used to pull munitions carts were wandering around in the haze. Some of the horses were so injured, guards shot them to put the poor animals out of their misery.

I could imagine huge horses, their heads hanging down, their eyes half closed, frightened by the sounds of the explosions but too weak to drag themselves through the smoke. My heart broke. I sat down on the last step crying like a baby. Tears and sobs just came on like a thunderstorm—all for poor, defenseless horses. It's not right to cry for the horses when people died too. I just couldn't help it.

CHAPTER TWENTY

THE THEFT

The next morning, Dad took the Liberty Loan money to the bank. "I'll be back in fifteen minutes." He stuffed a small bag of cash into his coat pocket. "Watch the store for me." He motioned for me to come to the back door. "When you're alone in the store, keep this door locked."

"Sure." I turned the key and hung it on the nail on the door molding.

Dad was gone a short time when I heard the front-door bell jingle. Billy Detwiler came in rubbing his eye.

Trying to live up to Dad's trust in me, I kept my feelings in check and gave Billy our standard customer greeting. "Hello, Billy. How can I help you?" His eye was red and swollen. *Had someone punched him?*

Billy blinked a few times and rubbed his eye. "I think I have a cinder in my eye." Cinders were a regular problem since side streets weren't paved, but instead just dirt and rocks or cinder-covered.

"Don't rub it," I said. "That will make things worse. Have you tried blowing your nose?"

Billy looked at me as if I were an idiot. "Why would I blow my nose? The cinder's in my eye."

"Blowing your nose will make your eye water and maybe the cinder will wash out," I said.

"You're making that up."

Smart Alec. "Why didn't you go home and have your mother take care of it?"

"Your store was closer." He pulled a handkerchief out of his pocket. "So, blowing my nose is going to get this cinder out?"

I nodded. "It might."

Billy blew his nose. He blinked. "I can still feel it."

"Try again."

"Maybe you should look at my eye in the back of the store where there's more light," Billy suggested.

That was exactly what my father would have done. Customers had gone to the back of the store a hundred times for this, but I hesitated. I still had my suspicions about Billy and the attempted theft on Labor Day. "I think we should wait for my dad."

Billy kept blowing his nose. "It's not working, Josie. What else can you do?" He held his hand over his eye. "I can't wait for your father. The pain is killing me."

"He should be here any minute."

"I could go blind," Billy pleaded.

I waved Billy to the back of the store and sat him on the stool by the window. I tried to stand where I could still see the mirror and the front of the store.

"Over here, Josie. The light is brighter." He slid the stool closer to the window, but now I couldn't see out front.

"Where is the cinder? Under the upper lid or the lower?"

"Upper."

After I washed my hands, I put my finger on his eyebrow and gently pulled the eyelid up. I couldn't see anything.

"Look again," he said.

Then I carefully pulled the lower lid down the same way. "I can't see anything, Billy."

Billy kept blinking. "I think it's moving around."

What else might Dad do? "Try this. Pull your upper lid out and over the lower lid. The cinder might catch on your lower lashes."

"That won't work," he said.

Why was Billy being so thick? I made Billy try several times.

As Billy clumsily worked at bringing the upper lid over the bottom one, there was a thump from the front of the store. "What was that?" I asked, but everything was quiet. When I tried to go out front to see, Billy grabbed my arm.

"Josie, there's nobody there. What else can we try?"

"Well, I've seen my Dad use a cotton swab or the corner of a clean handkerchief."

"Try that," Billy urged. "Anything to get this cinder out." He frowned, his bottom lip sticking out. "It hurts bad, Josie. You gotta help me."

"I don't want to touch your eye with anything," I said. "If I accidently poke your eye, it would be worse."

Billy still held my arm.

"We could try eyewash," I said. "I have to get it from the front."

Billy wouldn't let go of my arm. He looked frightened.

"I'm just going out front to get some eyewash. You'll be all right. Try not to blink too much, and *don't* rub it."

The shop bell jingled, and the screen door slammed. "Maybe that's Dad," I said.

Still cupping his eye with his hand, Billy got up and came with me to the front of the store.

No Dad. No anyone. "I thought I heard the bell."

"I didn't hear any bell," Billy said.

The eyewash was on a high shelf, so I needed the stepstool to reach it. As I got the bottle, I heard the shop bell ring yet again. I turned to look and saw Billy outside walking away. Wasn't that just like Billy Detwiler to leave and not even thank anyone! Irritated, I shoved the eyewash back on the shelf and climbed down.

What is this? A crumpled piece of paper lay on the floor. I opened it to see my map. My store map that Miss Penny couldn't find. A red arrow pointed to—*the stamp drawer.* I ran to check the post office counter. A crowbar lay on the floor, and the stamp drawer hung open as if dangling by a thread. The Labor Day thief was back. And Billy had been in the store.

Dad! I needed Dad! Now I was the one hightailing it out of the store. On the sidewalk I skidded to a halt. Thank goodness, Dad was coming up the street. I yelled for him to hurry. Billy was nowhere to be seen.

Dad arrived at a quick trot. "Josie, what's wrong?"

"Did you just see Billy Detwiler leave the store?" I asked.

"No."

I dragged Dad by the hand inside.

"What's happened?" he asked, sounding alarmed. We rounded the post office counter. "What's this crowbar?"

I pointed to the demolished stamp drawer.

"Damn!" He bent down and held my shoulders. "Are you all right? Did anyone hurt you?"

"No, no one hurt me." I blinked back tears. Dad had trusted me to watch the store, and I had been foolish enough to let Billy Detwiler trick me into taking him to the back of the pharmacy.

Dad held me and said, "It's all right, Josie. There, there. As long as you are not hurt. It's all right." He patted my back.

There was a loud bang. We both flinched. It was the drawer finally falling onto the floor.

Dad assessed the damage. "They got some money," he said. "Luckily it wasn't much." He moved papers around, searching. "What else is missing?" He looked around on the floor and back at the drawer contents. "Blast it! They took the revolver too."

"Ohhh Daddy, I'm so sorry." I covered my mouth with my fingers. "It's my fault. I was in the back with Billy Detwiler."

My father's eyebrows flew to the top of his head. "What?"

"Billy had a cinder in his eye, and his eye was all red and he kept rubbing it, and I thought I could help him." Getting sent home from school for kicking Billy was nothing compared to how I felt now. My mouth was dry and my knees were shaking.

"Slow down. Tell me everything."

I gave Dad a full accounting.

"And you think Billy was involved because . . . ?"

I explained how Billy stopped me from going out front.

"Billy was not behind the post office counter," Dad said. "And you did not see him with the gun."

"Yes, but—"

"It's possible he was a decoy," Dad said. "And he had help."

"Could it have been those Mackenzie boys?" I asked.

Dad shrugged. "What worries me more is the possibility the gun is in the hands of children."

A loaded gun. I had let Dad down, and now someone might be accidently shot.

Dad called the constable, and I told the story several more times, but the constable thought there wasn't enough information to hold Billy responsible. As long as Billy was with me when it happened and was nowhere near the stamp drawer, there wasn't much he could do for now. "I'll talk to Mrs. Detwiler, because ironically, Billy is the only other witness," the constable said.

What had I been thinking? "Daddy, I'm sorry. I should have known better."

Dad scratched the back of his neck. "Josie, what do you think I would have done if Billy came in the store with a red, swollen eye, saying he had a cinder in it?"

I chewed my lip.

"I would have helped Billy just as you did," Dad said.

"But I should have waited for you to return."

"You could have. And in hindsight, that would have been the better choice," Dad agreed. "What's done is done. Now we have to deal with finding the revolver before anyone gets hurt."

☙

Later that night as I lay in bed, I heard the constable talking in our kitchen. I could have predicted what he was going to say. Mrs. Detwiler was livid that anyone would suspect her precious Billy of having anything to do with stealing anything, let alone a gun. She had no idea who the Mackenzie boys were, and she doubted her son would be so stupid as to take up with two thieves.

Dear God, Help the constable find the gun. Don't let anyone get hurt. I stared at the ceiling. The kitchen clock struck nine. I tried sleeping on my stomach. I fluffed my pillow. The clock struck ten. My stomach felt like ants had built a nest in it. The clock chimed ten-fifteen. I tried sleeping on my side.

Before Gram climbed into bed, she gave me a little kiss on the forehead.

"'Night, Grandma," I whispered.

"Good night, Josie. Tomorrow will be better."

I heard my parents talking upstairs in their bedroom, but I couldn't make out what they were saying. The house settled. Mother coughed. *Why did I help Billy Detwiler?* Hadn't Grace and I both agreed we'd never trust him farther than we could spit? The clock struck eleven. I wondered if Dad would ever let me help him in the store after today.

∾

Incredibly, Dad had me helping in the store the next morning. Mr. Gardener came in wearing one of the gauze masks we'd given him on Monday. Grace was not with him.

"Hello, Joe," Mr. Gardener said through the gauze.

"Liberty Bonds are selling fairly well."

"Glad to hear it, but I'm not here about that. I'm here to get some things for Grace. She came down with the flu last night."

My heart skipped a beat. *Grace has influenza?*

Mr. Gardener wondered aloud where Grace could have picked up flu.

Grace had only been at home or at our store in the past week. And at the parade. What if she caught it here? Should I tell about Grace sneaking off to the parade? No one likes a tattletale. And if I tell, would Grace get in trouble for disobeying her parents? What kind of friend tattles on her best friend? *Fiddlesticks!*

Be helpful, Josie, I told myself. Do something good. I helped Dad make a package of things Grace would need. At lunch I asked Mother if I could make Jell-O for Grace.

"We'll make soup too," she said.

Worries nagged me the rest of the afternoon. How sick was Grace? Did she catch it here? But Grace had not been upstairs or near my mother. What about George and Frank? Should I tell about their going to the parade?

Tiny couldn't cut out paper doll clothes without turning them into a mess. As I snipped I thought, *I'm sick of this.* I'm sick of people getting sick. I'm sick of the Kaiser and Billy Detwiler. I'm sick of chicken soup. I'm sick of my hands being chapped and sore from washing everything. What happened to a simple little cold cured by bed rest, gallons of tea, and tender loving care?

Curses! I cut right through a paper tab.

I lost my patience for paper dolls. I scolded Tiny for making too much noise and made her play outside.

Trees in the backyard were yellow and orange and leaves had started falling, but not enough for a good leaf pile.

"Keep your sweater on," I called to my sister. "It's not that hot out."

Tiny stuck her tongue out and left her sweater unbuttoned.

☙

By late afternoon, raspberry Jell-O had gelled in little glass dishes, chicken soup had cooled in Mason jars, and I had played "school" with Tiny until I thought she was ready for college. I was anxious to see Grace. "Mother, may I take the soup and jellies over now?"

Mother and Gram consulted one another. Under no circumstances was I to go inside the Gardeners' apartment. I was to leave the soup outside the door. Gram helped me put the jars and jellies in a box. Mother tucked a note to Mrs. Gardener among the towels we used for padding in between the jars and dishes. At the last minute I put two books in for Grace to read.

Like us, Grace's family lived in the apartment above her father's shop. Upstairs, Frank met me at the kitchen door.

I pulled the gauze mask over my nose. "I brought Grace some Jell-O and soup."

Frank nodded. "I hope you have a lot. George is sick too."

"Oh no."

"Do your parents know about the parade?" Frank whispered through the screen door.

I shook my head no.

He kept his voice low. "Neither one of those two birdbrains kept their masks on while we were at the parade. Nobody had masks on. Everyone crammed to see the marchers and the floats. A man standing behind Grace sneezed right on her." Frank shook his head. "We should never have gone. Now both of them are sick because of me."

Desperate for something good to say, I told Frank, "If Grace eats right and stays in bed, she'll get better. So will George."

"Thank you, Josie." But his weak smile said he was just as worried as I was.

At home, Mother was lying down, and Tiny's paper dolls were all over the kitchen table. "How's Grace?" Gram asked.

"She was sleeping. George is sick too." *Should I tell? Tell about the parade?*

Gram shook her head. "That's a shame. Mary will really have her hands full with two sick children."

While I helped Dad in the store, Doctor Fagan came in. "Gravediggers can't keep up with the burials, and twenty coffins are waiting at St. Peter's Cemetery."

Those are not empty coffins. A chill went down my spine.

Doc Fagan wrote out prescriptions. "They're organizing an isolation hospital for influenza cases in New Brunswick. It's about time. Quarantine's still in effect."

Grace's father came to the store.

"How are we doing?" Dad asked.

"Do you mean the Liberty Loan or the kids?" Mr. Gardener answered. "Highland Park's doing well, but overall, the loan is behind schedule. Influenza is hampering things, and with the recent peace talks, maybe people don't think it's as important to subscribe this time." He turned to the doctor. "I'm glad you're here. The kids have wicked headaches, and the aspirin doesn't seem to be working. Frank's sick too."

Frank too? The older brother I wish I had.

"Phenocoll?" Dad asked Doctor Fagan.

While Dad counted out tablets, Mr. Gardener told us that Frank had been delirious during the night and talked about how he had gone over to the parade with George and Grace.

They know. I wondered if the Gardeners were cross with their children. I hoped not. Flu was punishment enough.

CHAPTER TWENTY-ONE

NO MAN'S LAND AT MRS. DETWILER'S

Dear Grace,

Are you feeling better? How are Frank and George? It feels funny not going to church and school, doesn't it? Doctor Fagan told me it might be a few more weeks until the quarantine is lifted. I might go crazy staying at home. Are you well enough to eat ice cream yet? Let me know, and I will bring you some. W. B.

Love,

Josie

I dropped my note to Grace at her house when I delivered papers. Mrs. Gardener told me through the screen door that Grace and her brothers were the same. Weak, feverish, coughing. At least they weren't worse.

Sunday's edition was lighter than usual. So many newspaper workers were sick with flu they had to cut the

Sunday paper down to eight pages. I read the headlines as I turned onto Adelaide Avenue. Germany was accepting President Wilson's peace terms, but officials were skeptical about the Germans' real intentions. Could the war really be ending or were the Germans playing tricks?

Adelaide Avenue had big houses and carefully spaced, mature trees that arched into a colorful canopy. The only thing wrong with Adelaide Avenue was that Billy lived here. I still couldn't shake the belief that he was behind the theft of Dad's gun.

As I brought the paper up to his front porch, there was Billy sitting on the front step. Behind him the front door stood ajar. I handed him the paper, but he wouldn't take it. He didn't say anything. He wasn't even trying to be rude. What was wrong?

Mrs. Detwiler called from inside, *"Wilhelm. Wilhelm. Ich brauche dich."* I couldn't understand what she said, but she sounded pitiful.

"Is that your mother?" I asked.

Billy sat there like a rock.

"Help me," came from inside the door. Then there was a crash, the sound of furniture falling, and a thud.

"Billy, I think your mother fell!"

Billy still did not move.

I held my face mask across my nose and mouth and pushed the door open. Mrs. Detwiler lay on the floor.

There was blood on her sleeves and across the front of her nightgown. More blood flowed from the cut on her head where she must have hit the marble-topped table when she fell. Pink shards of glass from a broken lamp glistened on the floor and in her hair.

"What's wrong with your mother?" I gasped.

Billy was silent.

I grabbed his arm to get his attention and yelled, "What's happened to your mother? All this blood is not just from her head!"

I yanked him to his feet. Billy stared at his mother through the door.

Mrs. Detwiler started moaning, *"Mutter, Mutter."*

"What's she saying?"

"Wer ist da? Ist es Gisela?"

Holding the mask closer to my face, I knelt down and felt Mrs. Detwiler's forehead. She was burning. She coughed in between her sobs. Blood trickled from her mouth.

"Don't move, Mrs. Detwiler. Please stay still. We'll get help." I gently brushed shards of glass off her face.

"Helfen Sie mir. Oh Gott, vergib mir. Jesus hilf mir."

It sounded like gibberish. "Billy, what is she saying?" I didn't wait for an answer. I tried to help Mrs. Detwiler get up, but she was too heavy for me. "Billy, help me get your mother off the floor!"

"Are you an angel?" Mrs. Detwiler reached up and touched my face. She had the saddest eyes. They were glassy, like a doll's. *"Danke Gott."*

She lapsed into gibberish again. Delirium could do that.

"Don't tell, Josie," Billy said.

Don't tell? Was he serious? "Don't tell what?"

"My mother speaks German," he said. "No one must know." He sounded desperate.

"Billy, there's no time for that! We have to hurry and get your mother some help. She's bleeding!"

He stepped toward the doorway and hesitated.

"Billy, your mother could be dying! Take her shoulders and I'll get her feet. We have to pick her up."

Mrs. Detwiler was a dead weight. We would never be able to get her up the stairs to her bed. "Let's put her on the couch . . . Wait . . . Put her down and stay here. Where does your mother keep her sheets? The linen closet?"

He nodded vaguely. "Upstairs."

I ran upstairs and found the closet. Grabbing sheets and a blanket, I thought, *Pillow. She'll need a pillow.* I grabbed one from her bed. Clearly, Mrs. Detwiler had been sick for several days. The pillows and sheets had blood on them. Dirty glasses and cups filled the top of the night table along with open bottles of aspirin and cough medicine. Used and bloody handkerchiefs were piled on the floor. On the way back down, I got a clean pillowcase and some washcloths and found some gauze and bandages in the bathroom. Downstairs I threw a sheet on the sofa, and Billy and I half-dragged and half-carried Mrs. Detwiler to the couch and somehow got her on it.

"Call my father," I said as I stuffed the pillow in the clean pillowcase. "The number's three-four-five."

Mrs. Detwiler's forehead was still bleeding. I put several gauze bandages on the wound. Heat radiated from her forehead. I didn't need a thermometer to tell she had a raging fever.

As I picked glass from her hair and clothing, I could hear Billy in the hallway. "Hello? Hello? Operator?" There must have been no answer because I could hear him clicking the earpiece cradle up and down. *The telephone company must still be short-handed because of the flu.* No one was taking his call. I heard him yell from the hall, "Hello! Hello!" And then I heard him curse and slam the earpiece down on the cradle.

He came back in the living room and clenched the end of the sofa. "She's going to die, isn't she?"

"No, no," I lied. But I thought she might die right here and now. "Here, put this other sheet over her."

Billy did as I said.

"Get some ice," I said, "for her forehead."

He hesitated. "I can't."

"All right. I'll get the ice, and you hold this bandage on her head."

"I don't think we have any ice," he said. "I think she used it all."

I handed him one of the washcloths. "Okay, just make this cold. Let the water run awhile so it's really cold."

Billy came back with the cold washcloth. I put it on Mrs. Detwiler's forehead.

"*Gisela…Gisela. Gott sie Dank, du bist hier.*" Mrs. Detwiler was babbling again.

"Billy, do you understand what your mother is saying? Is Gisela a name?"

"She thinks you're her sister."

I held Mrs. Detwiler's hand. "It's me, Mrs. Detwiler, Josie Winslow. Billy and I are trying to help you."

Mrs. Detwiler started thrashing her arms. For a minute, I thought she was reacting to me, her least favorite person in the world. I tried to hold her arms down, but it was useless. In her state, she accidently tore my influenza mask off my face. I tried to put it back on, but the ties had ripped out.

"*I'm so cold,*" she said, her teeth chattering, her body shaking.

I readjusted the sheet. Mrs. Detwiler continued to shiver and talk half in German and half in English. I added a blanket.

Mrs. Detwiler looked awful. Her cheeks were bright red from the fever. She had dried blood on her cheek and forehead. I used the cold compress to try to wipe some of it away. My own hands had blood on them. Mrs. Detwiler coughed again. This time I could feel spittle on my face.

"I need to get my father," I said.

"Don't leave me alone, Josie," Billy pleaded. "I don't know what to do."

"Okay, you get my father," I said.

Billy ran out the door, and Mrs. Detwiler quieted down.

I looked at the bloody washcloth in my hands. How many times had my parents instructed me not to go into houses because of the flu? And here I was sitting on Gretchen Detwiler's coffee table, without even a mask, and covered in blood. *I'm in more trouble,* I thought. Then it hit me, Dad was not home. He was at a funeral on the north side of town. For a minute I panicked. *I've sent Billy on a wild goose chase. Think, Josie,* I reminded myself. *What will Mother do? She'll tell Billy where to find Dad and Billy can run over to Grant Avenue. It will take longer but it will work out.* All I could do was hope.

The compress was warming up, so I went to the kitchen to make it cold again. The kitchen was a disaster. No one had washed dishes in days. I had to stretch to open the door of the icebox because a puddle of water was seeping out from the catch pan underneath it. I checked the ice container on top. No ice. It had all melted.

At least I could try to make Mrs. Detwiler comfortable. I found a dishpan under the sink and clean dish towels in a drawer. It felt awkward going through someone else's kitchen, especially Mrs. Detwiler's. It was a good thing she was prostrate on the sofa, because if she knew I had been through her closets and her kitchen, she'd have had a stroke. I filled the dishpan with water from the tap and took the tub and the towels back to the living room.

After I put the new compress on Mrs. Detwiler's forehead, I washed her hands and face, trying not to disturb the blood-soaked gauze on her forehead. For now the bleeding had stopped.

"Gisela, du bist so nett." Mrs. Detwiler was talking in German again.

"English, Mrs. Detwiler, please talk to me in English so I can understand you."

"Thank you. Thank you. I think I might die. If I die, will you take Wilhelm?"

She still thinks I'm her sister, I thought.

"Don't worry about Billy," I said. "We will take care of him."

As I held her hand, I thought, *This is crazy. Now I am telling Mrs. Detwiler I will look after Billy.*

"Gisela, my mouth is so dry. Please get me a drink."

At least she was speaking English again.

Back in the kitchen, I hunted through cabinets for a clean glass. Luckily Mrs. Detwiler had far more glassware and china than she needed.

I helped Billy's mother sit up and propped the pillow behind her. "Just sips, all right?"

"You are a dear." She could barely talk. She took a swallow.

A dear? I was certain she still had no idea who I really was.

"Billy went for help," I said.

"Good God, my head aches." Mrs. Detwiler felt her forehead and groaned when she touched the bandage. "I feel a little dizzy." She tried to take another swallow of water, but her coughing started again. This time it wouldn't stop. Had she swallowed wrong? I took the water from her. She kept coughing, choking, or both. I tried to pound on her back in case she was choking. That didn't do any good. She coughed so hard she brought up more blood. Now her nightgown was soaked. I didn't dare leave her.

201

"Josie?"

I heard footsteps in the hallway.

"Is anyone home?"

I recognized Fred's voice.

"Don't come in," I hollered. "Mrs. Detwiler has the flu."

But it was too late. Fred and Tony stood at the doorway to the living room. They pulled up their masks.

"Holy cow!" Fred gasped.

"We saw your newspaper bag on the porch," Tony said. "And when we saw the door open and heard you talking . . . "

"I've never seen anyone so sick," Fred said.

"I have." Tony was somber. "Where's Billy?"

"I sent him to get my father."

"Do you want us to do anything?" Tony asked.

"Just watch her," I said, and I ran upstairs to Mrs. Detwiler's room. Once I had a fresh nightgown, I grabbed the medicines next to her bed and brought them downstairs. I showed the bottles to Mrs. Detwiler. "When did you take medicine last? At breakfast?"

She didn't remember. She seemed so sick, I wondered if it was the flu, a concussion, or an overdose. Or maybe all three. I wished my father would hurry.

"Can we help?" Fred asked. "I see Mrs. Detwiler has a bandage on her head. I could finish that."

"No," I said. "You can't risk coming in here."

"But I'm over the flu now," Fred said.

"Well, you could fill this basin with clean water," I suggested. "And make this towel cold."

Once Fred brought the water, I bathed Mrs. Detwiler's face again. This time I could see where the broken glass had cut her face. Mrs. Detwiler seemed to be sleeping. At least I hoped that's what she was doing. I replaced the washcloth on her forehead with a colder one.

For a moment everything was quiet. I heard the mantel clock tick between Mrs. Detwiler's labored breaths. She sounded raspy and gurgly.

"At least her lips aren't blue," Tony said, standing at the foot of the sofa.

"What's taking Billy so long?" Fred asked, and he went out to look for Billy or my father.

The clock ticked. Mrs. Detwiler coughed and mumbled in her sleep. I wondered if Tony would pick up Mrs. Detwiler's German.

"It's Billy." Fred reported from the porch.

Billy rushed into the house. "Your father is at Mr. Adams's house for the funeral. Your grandmother is coming." Billy looked helpless. "She said she would get a few things from the store and she'd be here."

"I know where Mr. Adams lives," Tony said. "I'll get Mr. Winslow."

"And I'll try to find Doctor Fagan," Fred said, and they took off.

Billy sat in the chair next to the sofa and stared at his mother.

I didn't have the heart to ask him why he hadn't gone to get my father at the funeral. He looked frightened and sad. How could he be the same kid who scared me with his bullying? Or the same kid I thought had stolen the gun from Dad's store?

I bathed Mrs. Detwiler's face again. Now that Fred and Tony were gone, I could change her nightgown.

"She's going to die," Billy said. "Tony's mother died."

"Try not to think that. Here, help me change this nightgown."

He looked at me as if I were crazy.

"Well, just close your eyes when we get to those parts."

It was a struggle, but we got the clean nightgown on Mrs. Detwiler.

"Okay, you can open your eyes now," I said. I wondered if I should try to keep him busy.

"We'll need to put that blood-stained nightgown in cold water to soak." It was Gram. She put down a large paper bag on the coffee table.

Thank goodness!

Gram came closer, and all I could do was hug her. "You shouldn't have come," I said. "You'll get sick."

"Oh, and now who's talking!" she chided. "I guess the apple doesn't fall far from the tree. This family just can't resist throwing themselves into the line of fire." She felt Mrs. Detwiler's forehead and took cardboard ice cream containers out of the bag. "Billy told me you didn't have ice." She tucked the smaller containers under each of Mrs. Detwiler's armpits. "Billy, do you have an ice bag in the house?"

Billy sat glassy-eyed in the chair next to the sofa.

"Maybe there's one in the bathroom," I said and headed upstairs to get it. As I came back down, I heard a car screech to a halt in front of the house. It was Doc Fagan and Dad. Tony and Fred hopped out of the back seat.

Doctor Fagan examined Mrs. Detwiler. "Call the hospital," he said, folding his stethoscope and putting it in his bag. "I hope there's room for her."

While Dad waited for an operator, Doctor Fagan bundled Mrs. Detwiler in the sheet and blanket. "You're probably not going to like this, Gretchen," he said, "but we're taking you to the hospital."

Mrs. Detwiler was in no condition to argue.

CHAPTER TWENTY-TWO

DEATH NOTICE

On Monday I wrote Grace about Mrs. Detwiler and Billy. A neighbor, Mrs. Krumblebine, had offered to take care of Billy, and she told us that Billy's father worked for the military in Maryland, testing artillery shells. No wonder Billy had such a fascination with things that could blow up. But if Mr. Detwiler was engaged in war work, I doubted if he could come home.

Dad came in the kitchen. "Telegram from Billy's aunt. She'll be here tomorrow."

I wondered when we would hear from Mr. Detwiler.

I was folding Grace's note when Mother screamed from upstairs. "Oh God! No!" She tore down the stairs and into the kitchen.

"What on earth?" Gram exclaimed. "What's happened?"

"Quackenboss's hearse is out front!" Mother cried.

Gram's jaw dropped. "Where?"

"Gardener's!" Mother bolted out the back door.

Gram ran after her. Dad and I were right on their heels.

"Is it Grace?" I yelled after them.

"I don't know!" Mother was already on the stairs to the Gardener's apartment. "Mary! Mary!" Mother shouted as she dashed inside.

As Gram and I followed, Dad held me back. "You can't go in."

Through the door, I saw Mrs. Gardener sobbing in my mother's arms. *Is it Grace?* I wondered.

"I want to come too," a little voice piped from the bottom of the stairs. Tiny had followed us.

"Keep her away from here," Dad said.

I waited at the bottom of the stairs with Tiny.

Mr. Quackenboss, the funeral director, escorted Mr. Gardener out the back door. Grace's mother cried, "Wait! I want to go with you!"

"What about Grace and George?" Mr. Gardener asked.

Now everyone was on the porch at the top of the stairs. "Get your things, Mary," Mother said. "We'll stay with the children while you make the arrangements."

Grace and George. Then it was Frank. Frank had died. I felt numb. Frank? Hadn't I just seen him on

Thursday? When he was worried about Grace and George . . . When he seemed fine . . . And wasn't it only Friday that Mr. Gardener told us Frank had come down with the flu? What happened? How could Frank die so fast?

Doctor Fagan stepped outside onto the porch with Dad. "Grace and George are too sick to even know what's going on." He did a little backbend and gazed at the sky. "Joe, I'll say it again and again. I just don't understand why this damn influenza kills the young and the healthy. And so fast."

As Grace's parents came down the stairs with Mr. Quackenboss, Mrs. Gardener stopped and hugged me. "Josie, you pray. You pray for George and Gracie, okay?" She touched Tiny's cheek. "And stay home. We don't want you to be sick too."

"We will," I said.

Mother and Gram stayed the rest of the day at Grace's house. Dad and I made supper. None of us were hungry. Especially Tiny. She didn't even want ice cream for dessert.

In bed I remembered how I felt when Tony's mother died. I cried and prayed. It was hard to believe Frank was gone. Not just for the day at school. Not off to college and home for Thanksgiving. Just gone. We'd never see him again. Would Grace or George be next? I cried so much my throat hurt, and I had a headache. He was so nice. I wondered if Grace even knew her brother was dead.

҈

The next morning, my sister came padding into the kitchen and climbed on Mother's lap. Tiny's teeth were chattering.

"She's shivering," Mother said, feeling Tiny's forehead. "And she's running a fever." Mother's face turned the color of skimmed milk.

Gram said, "Let's see how bad it is. Josie, get the thermometer."

Tiny held remarkably still with the thermometer in her mouth while we waited for the verdict.

"It's 104," Gram said.

"It can't be," Mother said. "It can't be flu!" She hugged Tiny closer.

"Ethel," Gram said. "Stay calm. You'll frighten Tiny. Let's see if she's hungry."

But she wasn't. Neither cinnamon toast nor hot chocolate could tempt her. My sister just sat limply in my mother's arms, her head draped on Mother's shoulder.

I thought about Frank. In three days he had died. Would Tiny be gone too by the weekend? What if we all catch it and we can't stop it? My stomach tied itself into a knot.

210

"We need to get busy," Gram said. "We can't fall apart now."

It didn't take long to marshal our defenses. I cleaned up breakfast, and Mother called Dr. Fagan. We isolated Tiny on the sofa in the living room. Someone would sleep in the chair so Tiny wouldn't be alone. The main idea was to keep Tiny away from me.

What would we do when everyone else became sick? Or died?

After Mother and Gram finished tucking Tiny into the makeshift bed, Mother sank into the chair and stared at my little sister. Tears streamed down Mother's cheeks.

"You need to be strong for Tiny," Gram said. "You need to take care of yourself. Relapse is still a danger."

Mother nodded, but her face contorted in despair. "Poor Mary and Frank," she said through her tears.

I knew I shouldn't do it, but I went into the room and knelt next to my mother. "It will be all right, Momma. You got better. Tiny will too." But I knew that it was just as likely Tiny could die.

"Oh Josie." Now Mother hugged me tightly. "I can't have both of you sick. I can't lose either of you! Promise me you'll stay away from your sister!"

☙

That evening we saw Frank's obituary in the paper.

Death Notice

Frank Gardener Jr., aged 17 of Highland Park. Young Mr. Gardener was a popular honor student at New Brunswick High School where he lettered in football and track. Frank volunteered as a junior fireman with the Highland Park Fire Department. He died peacefully in his sleep after a short bout with Spanish influenza. Funeral services will be Wednesday at 2:00 at the Quackenboss Funeral Home on Livingston Avenue.

❧

Later that night, I got up to use the bathroom. I peeked in the sitting room. Gram was asleep in the chair. Dad sat on the sofa next to my sister. He was bent over with his elbows on his knees, his hands holding his forehead. *He's praying for Tiny. He's afraid Tiny will die.* "Daddy, is Tiny all right?" I whispered.

He nodded. "Sleep, Josie. Keep your resistance up."

"I will, Daddy."

But sleep would not come. Frank had died, despite good health and good care. And Dad's praying made me worry more about Tiny. *She can't die. Not like Frank. Mother had pulled through.* I wondered if prayer worked if you were not on your knees. I slipped out of bed and knelt on the floor. "Dear God, please, hear my father's prayer, even if he forgot to get on his knees. Please help Tiny and Grace and George to get well. Please don't let them die."

࿇

Dad was the only one from our family who could go to Frank's funeral. Gram stayed with Grace and George, who were still too sick to leave the house. Mother stayed with Tiny. I wanted to go, but no one would let me. I wrote Grace another note, but I had yet to hear back.

࿇

Thursday came and Tiny still could not get out of bed. Mother napped upstairs—doctor's orders—and Gram took food to Grace's mother. I wondered how Grace was doing.

Gram wasn't gone long when I heard Tiny calling from the sofa.

"Gramma?" Tiny called. She sounded so stuffed up. "Gramma, I need to pee."

I hesitated. No one wanted me near a contagious Tiny. "Can it wait? Gram is next door. She'll be back soon," I said. But I knew Tiny could not wait. I grabbed a gauze mask and went to help my sister.

As I carried Tiny into the bathroom, her whole body felt hot in my arms. Was her temperature worse?

"Josie, I can't breathe."

"Here." I held a clean handkerchief over Tiny's nose. "Blow gently."

213

She blew and coughed. Specks of blood peppered the now full handkerchief. I threw the soiled hankie into a bucket of water and disinfectant under the sink.

Once I laid her back in bed, I gave Tiny the cherry-flavored water that was on the side table. I adjusted the straw to make it easier to sip. "You need to drink." *And I thought how awful it would be for such a little thing to die.*

‌ℯ

That night Dad didn't finish in the store until almost nine o'clock. I was already in bed, trying to read. He poked his head inside the door, wiggled his fingers at me, and disappeared back into the kitchen. I could hear him talking. "Paper said *eleven* more people died. Imagine eleven in one day. And there's talk of lifting the quarantine."

Eleven? That's nearly half my class. Eleven more coffins stacked and waiting to go in the ground. Would Frank's make that an even dozen?

"How can they lift the quarantine if so many people are still dying?" I called out.

Dad appeared at the door and stopped to yawn. "It's the number of new cases that will determine if we need to stay under quarantine."

I knew of four new cases since Friday. Billy. His mother. Frank had died. And the fourth new case was right in my own

214

house. Just thinking about it gave me a chill and a headache.

But the shivering and the headache got worse. Was this what Grace and her brothers went through? It was worse than when I had the measles last year. Worse than anything. By midnight I was sick to my stomach. I lay on the bathroom floor hoping the vomiting was over.

❧

I woke up again.

"How do you feel?" Dad asked.

"Awful."

"Want to try some ice chips?"

I shook my head. The pounding in my head started all over again.

❧

Someone took a washcloth off my forehead. I was still on the floor in the bathroom. There a pillow under my head and a sheet covered my body. I tried to sit up.

Gram rinsed the washcloth out in the sink. "Ready to go back to bed?" she asked.

She helped me get up to sit on the commode.

"My head still aches." I was afraid I'd get sick again.

"As soon as you can keep something down, we can give you aspirin." She walked me back to bed and gave me a sliver of ice on a spoon. It stayed down.

☙

When I awoke this time, early morning light filtered into the room. It hurt to even look around. The ice chips next to my bed had melted. I tried to sip the water, but as I sat up, my head felt like a boulder rolling off my shoulders. I flopped back into the pillow. I ached all over. My eyeballs throbbed. Even my eyelashes hurt — each and every one.

☙

"We haven't seen much gastritis with the flu, but as you well know, headaches can upset a delicate stomach." Doctor Fagan's thumb and forefinger gently held my wrist, taking my pulse. He pressed my fingernails. "Nice and pink — no cyanosis." He put the stethoscope earpieces in his ears and helped me sit up so he could listen to my heart and lungs. He thumped around my back. His fingers felt like little hammers. "Say 'ahhhh.'" The tongue depressor made me gag and that started me coughing. He helped me lie back. "I know, everything hurts."

☙

I heard Gram in the kitchen. I tried to take another sip of the ice water and discovered plain water had become flat ginger ale. My nose was so congested that it was hard to swallow and breathe at the same time.

&

Billy Detwiler tied a tourniquet around my head. He twisted the bandage tighter and held it while he stopped to read the directions. He kept twisting and twisting to make it tighter and tighter.

"Billy! Stop! You're cutting off her circulation!" Frank yelled.

I struggled, but the words stayed in my head and I couldn't move.

"You should blow your nose," Billy said.

"No, you should blow your nose!" I hollered back.

Frank put his hand on my forehead. It was remarkably gentle.

&

"That was some dream," Gram whispered, straightening the blankets on my bed.

"I was dreaming about Billy Detwiler and Frank."

"Shhsh. Tiny's sleeping."

I looked over at the big bed. "Is Tiny better?" I asked in a small voice.

"Well enough that she doesn't have to stay in the living room."

"Gram, did you ever dream about a dead person?"

"When your grandfather died I dreamt about him almost every night. He was like a ghost haunting my dreams, but then I got used to it. I still dream about him now and then."

"When you dream about him, do you think he is trying to talk to you?"

"I don't know, Josie." Gram shook the thermometer to get the mercury to a lower point in the glass tube. "Let's take your temperature, and then maybe you can drink a little for me."

My head still hurt. My back ached. My legs ached. I wiggled my toes. My toenails hurt, but I think my heart hurt most of all.

Gram stuck the thermometer in my mouth. It was hard to breathe. and even harder not to cough.

"Try to keep your mouth closed," Gram reminded. "We won't get an accurate reading if you don't."

"I 'an't 'eathe," I mumbled, trying to keep my lips closed. I couldn't hold back the urge to cough any more. I could feel phlegm rumbling up from my chest with each stifled cough.

Gram grabbed the thermometer out of my mouth and helped me sit up. I coughed hard enough to bring up what seemed like a bucket of phlegm. Gram handed me a paper cup to spit in. The phlegm was a dark, yellowish-brown.

"Eewww," I said, coughing again. I had never hawked that much in my life.

Gram gently pounded my back with her fist. "Let's keep that mucus moving."

I obliged and coughed up more yellowy gunk into the cup

"That's what we call a productive cough," she said. "At least it's not red."

Red? I remembered what Dad said about Tony's mother. Before her lips turned blue, she had coughed up blood. Bubbly, frothy blood. Had Frank died the same way? And Grace. Was she any better or, I hesitated, worse?

"One hundred and two," Gram said. "And we didn't even leave the thermometer in long enough."

"Gram, how is Grace?" I asked.

"She and George are still very sick."

I blew my nose and flopped back on the pillow. Frank Gardener had died, Grace and George were not out of the woods, and Tiny was sick enough that my father had prayed over her. I looked at Tiny cuddled under the covers. What a relief. Gram thinks Tiny is improving.

I heard the clink of a spoon on china. Mother sat on Tiny's bed and whispered, "That's good, Clementine. Soon you'll get strong and then you can get up." She dabbed Tiny's lips with a napkin and turned to me. "Are you hungry yet?"

I shrugged. Exertion made me cough.

Quickly Mother handed me a sputum cup. Coughing up phlegm was exhausting. Everything was exhausting. Even taking a half a teaspoon of Brown Mixture was exhausting and unpleasant. It tasted awful, which was a good thing, since an overdose could kill you.

≈

"Ready for lunch?" Gram waited with a tray of something steaming.

I groaned as I sat up. I had coughed so much my ribs ached when I tried to move.

Mother came in with a tray for Tiny.

"Didn't Tiny already eat?" I asked.

"No." Mother sounded quizzical. "Maybe you're thinking of yesterday."

Yesterday? "What's today?" I asked.

"Tuesday," Mother said.

Like my mother, I had lost track of time. When did I first get sick? I counted on my fingers—Thursday night, Friday, Saturday, Sunday, Monday—

"Doctor Fagan says Grace and George are on the mend," Gram said.

I brightened.

She placed the tray on my lap. Soup. "What are these? They look like little worms," I said, poking curly white things with the spoon.

"Spaetzle. German noodles." Gram said. "Mrs. Detwiler's sister made the soup especially for you. She feels badly that you fell sick after helping Billy's mother."

I stirred the soup.

"Does Grace know about Frank?"

Gram nodded.

Poor Grace. Her poor family. I felt helpless. Billy's aunt had made me soup. What could I do for Grace and her family? Not much, sick as I was. Steam drifted upwards and made my nose run. I pushed the funny-looking noodles out of the way and saw perfectly square dices of carrots and chicken. I tasted a spoonful of broth. It was hot and good. The spaetzle fit on the spoon and slid easily down my throat. "Is Mrs. Detwiler all right?" I asked.

Gram nodded. "Yes. Billy is too."

"I'm not eating the worms," Tiny announced.

"See?" Mother pointed to me. "Josie is eating the noodles, so you can too. Open wide."

The next morning, Gram pulled two envelopes out of her apron pocket. There was a get well card with a picture of a sweet Scottie puppy on the front. To my surprise, it was from Billy's Aunt Gisela. *She's nice. Not*

like her sister. But then I felt bad because Mrs. Detwiler — or Billy — could have died. The second letter was from Grace.

Dear Josie,

I guess you know about Frank. I keep thinking I hear him, but it's just my imagination, I guess. My mother told me you and Tiny are sick with influenza too. Do everything Doctor Fagan tells you to do, so you can get better fast. Thank you for sending the notes. I wasn't able to read them right away. I was too sick, and my eyes ached too much to focus on anything. George is better, but we are all so in the dumps because of Frank. Mother and I take turns crying. When she cries, I just feel like I have to try to cheer her up, so I don't cry. I don't think my dad could take both of us crying at the same time. I guess you haven't felt up to writing since you got sick, but when you feel better, please keep writing. Doctor Fagan says it's good for me to have something to look forward to.

Love,

Grace

&

Friday morning we had soft-boiled eggs and toast. Tiny could have milk now. Her fever was down. I could hear Gram and Mother in the kitchen.

"Ethel, did you see in the paper there's a shortage of caskets?"

What do they do with dead people where there are no coffins? I pictured the coffins waiting in St. Peter's Cemetery. Did Frank have a coffin?

❧

"Good morning, Josie," Doctor Fagan said. "I see you are feeling well enough to read a little." He picked up the Ruth Fielding book that had slipped onto the floor.

I turned my head away and coughed into my handkerchief. "How are Grace and George?"

"They are coming along."

Hearing this made me feel better.

Dad watched as the doctor did his examination. "I heard the quarantine is lifted," Dad said. "Principal Springfield came by earlier and said New Brunswick is reopening schools on Monday. What do you think?"

Doctor Fagan reluctantly agreed that schools could reopen.

"Hallelujah!" I started to get out of bed.

"Oh, not so fast, Josie." Doc Fagan held me back. "You're still recuperating. You might be allowed out of bed in a day or so, but you'll have to stay in the house awhile longer.

Fiddlesticks!

❧

Instead of thinned-out milk on my oatmeal, there was cream on my cereal this morning! Hip! Hip! Hooray! Another sign things were improving.

Mother opened a window. "Let's air out this room. Do you want to sit in the chair for a while, Josie?"

From the chair, I could see that the trees on Raritan Avenue were now a blaze of yellow, red, and orange. There were enough leaves on the sidewalk that we'd have to start sweeping them into the gutter.

A breeze floated into the room. I was surprised at how warm it was for this late in October. It seemed like eons ago that we were eating tomatoes and peaches and I'd been in school.

Tiny got out of bed and climbed up on my lap.

"Aren't the leaves pretty, Tiny?" I said, pulling the sheer curtain away so we could see better. "Soon we'll be jumping in leaf piles. Won't that be fun?"

Gram came in the room shaking the thermometer. While she waited for my temperature to register, she felt Tiny's forehead. "You seem all right. Your breakfast is waiting in the kitchen."

I took the thermometer out and read it myself. "One hundred," I announced.

"Breakfast is waiting in the kitchen for you too."

At the table, Mother said the Tallman family finally got word about their son. "He's a prisoner of war.

At least he's alive, and when the war ends, he'll come home, thank God."

The war. No one had said a word about it in ages. "What did I miss? About the war. There's still a war on, you know," I mimicked Gram.

"Oh! Someone's feeling better!" Mother laughed.

"President Wilson's been sending messages back and forth with the Germans," Gram said. "We hoped the Germans would accept Wilson's terms, but then the Germans backed out because they couldn't agree on an armistice."

"And the Germans didn't want to stop submarine warfare," Mother added. "And they were miffed because someone accused them of cruelty to the countries they occupied. Oh, *ve* don't mean to be cruel," she said in a mock German accent. "*Vouldn't* all you folks in Belgium *vant* to be German too? Excuse us as *ve* march through your country, destroy your homes, and take all your food on our *vay* to France. Now everyone say '*Ja-vold*' or *ve'll* have to shoot you."

I was stunned. Mother had never said anything so sarcastic. I didn't know if I should laugh or not.

Mother returned to her normal voice. "We have to talk with the French and the English before answering the latest German memo."

"But the good news is the Germans are retreating from Antwerp and German soldiers are deserting," Gram said.

"Wilson sent representatives to Paris to work on negotiations, but not many people believe the Germans these days."

"Is there still fighting?" I asked.

Mother nodded.

More fighting meant more Meatless Mondays. No sugar. Miss Penny's beau still over there. And Dad could still be drafted.

CHAPTER TWENTY-THREE

RECUPERATION AND HALLOWEEN

Dear Grace,

Oh, how I wish we were in school today! Five-day rule. Dad said Dr. Fagan was doing the right thing—making any student who had recovered from the flu wait five days until they went back to school. But still. Fiddlesticks! I'm going crazy sitting in bed all day! This afternoon it's just Tiny and me. Mother and Gram are in the store. I lost weight while I was sick, and Mother wants me to gain it back, so I'm on an ice cream diet. I wish you could come up here and visit. Write back.

Love,

Josie

"Pssst. Josie." Grace stood in the doorway taking off her coat. She was wearing Frank's varsity sweater over her nightgown!

"What are you doing here?" I whispered.

"Your note said you wanted me to come over." She tiptoed over to my bed, put her coat and her school bag on the chair, and pulled out a pair of slippers. She rummaged around some more in the bag and produced two books. Grace whispered, "This was Doctor Fagan's idea." She handed me a book. "Another Ruth Fielding. I read it already, so you can borrow it." Grace unlaced her shoes and put on her slippers. Nestling up next to the window, she said, "Now we can recuperate together."

I gave Grace one of my pillows to lean on.

She thumped the pillow to get comfortable. "This one is about Ruth Fielding volunteering for the Red Cross in France." She paused, and her eyes got all big as she tapped her finger on the book's title. "It's about . . . *the war.*"

"Oh-ho! What's this?" Doctor Fagan stood at the doorway, a twinkle in his eye.

Mother was right behind the doctor, carrying a tray. "Looks like I need more ice cream," she said.

Tiny sat up in her bed. "Yay! Ice cream."

"Might as well check all three," the doctor said.

Doctor Fagan stuck a thermometer in Grace's mouth. "I see you took my suggestion."

He turned to Mother. "I thought good company would help speed recuperation," he explained. Then he gently chided Grace. "I thought we were going to start this tomorrow."

Grace bit her lip and the thermometer nearly fell out.

Doctor Fagan spoke to Mother. "What do you say to the two of them spending an hour together after lunch for a few days?"

"I think we can manage that." Mother served Tiny and gave my bowl of ice cream to Grace. "I'll get you some in a minute," she said to me.

"Barring any unforeseen circumstances," the doctor said, "I think you will both be in school on Monday."

I cheered. Grace smiled the best she could while holding the thermometer in her mouth. "Ah-ah," the doctor warned. "No over-exertion. You're supposed to be quiet."

❧

The next afternoon, Grace and I rocked in the chairs on the back porch. Doctor's orders. It was the first time I had been outside in over a week, and it was delightfully warm. Nearly seventy degrees.

"It's hard to believe it's this warm so close to Halloween," I said.

Grace rocked with her legs sticking straight out. "I don't feel much like Halloween."

I think Grace was missing her brother. She had brought Frank's sweater with her, but it was too warm to wear it again.

Dr. Fagan wanted me to try to interest Grace in doing things to help take her mind off Frank. "Well, if you *felt* like Halloween, what would you be?" I asked.

Grace shrugged.

"I might still fit into the cat costume," I thought aloud.

"Ghosts are always easy," Grace added. But then her face clouded.

Getting Grace's mind off Frank was going to be harder than I thought. "Maybe we're getting too old for Halloween," I said. "Halloween is for little kids like Tiny."

Grace stopped rocking.

What was she thinking?

"When I was little like Tiny, Frank and George dressed up like ghosts and snuck in my bedroom to scare me," Grace said.

I waited. "And?"

Her mouth made this funny half-smile, half-frown. And then she started crying and laughing at the same time. "Boy, did they get in trouble!"

I didn't know if I should laugh with her or cry.

Grace grabbed his sweater and buried her face in the wool. "I miss my brother," she sobbed. "He was so much fun."

"I'm sorry, Grace. I didn't mean to make you cry."

"It's okay. I know," she sniffed, trying to stop the stream of tears.

Gram came out on the porch to see what was wrong. "Frank was a fun-loving young man. It's good to remember him that way and the good times you had together. It's what we call bittersweet. I think Frank would want you to laugh."

After Gram went inside, Grace said, "Maybe you *should* have a little party for your sister. Carve a pumpkin and have some treats." She paused. "Don't spoil your fun on account of me."

It wouldn't be much fun without Grace.

"Now, what would we do for treats?" Grace asked. "Can't pull taffy—no sugar."

"We could have apple cider and donuts," I suggested. "We could bob for apples, too."

It almost felt like old times. "Do you want to help?"

"Nah," Grace said. "It wouldn't feel right."

"But Doctor Fagan wants—" I started.

"I'd just be an old wet blanket on your fun."

"If you change your mind . . . " I said hopefully.

∾

Halloween morning, Tiny and I rooted through the old clothes trunk for costumes. The Red Cross nurses' uniforms were on top. I was surprised my cape felt a little small. *Had I grown that much?*

"Where's the kitty cat?" Tiny asked, digging her way to the bottom of the trunk.

I grabbed her arms. "Hold still." I found the black material and gently pulled it out. "Here it is." The arms and legs were too long, and the tail would definitely drag on the ground, but Tiny was already taking off her clothes. Once Tiny had the black cat outfit on, she would not take it off. I rolled up the legs and the sleeves, and I fluffed the stuffed ears so they'd stand up. As I snapped the hood in place under her chin, Tiny meowed.

By evening Tiny was still dressed as the black cat, and apple cider and donuts waited on the kitchen table. My mouth watered as I thought about crunchy cinnamon sugar coating the outside of the donuts.

We heard footsteps on the stairs. It was Grace, and George was with her carrying a pumpkin. Grace swam in Frank's old fireman's uniform, and George's uniform was so tight he could hardly get his arms down.

"We thought Tiny might like a jack-o'-lantern," Grace said.

"You'll stay, won't you?" I asked.

"We could use some help carving the pumpkin," Gram said, motioning for Grace to sit down. "Especially, we can use your strong arms, George."

Gram made popcorn, and George scooped out the pumpkin to make the jack-o'-lantern. Tiny, Grace, and I separated seeds from the stringy pulp and got them ready for toasting. George let Tiny poke out the triangles and mouthparts he had carved to make the face. We lowered a lit candle into the pumpkin and turned off the lights. It was perfectly spooky.

I poured cider, and we helped ourselves to sugar-encrusted donuts and popcorn.

"This isn't a ghost story," Mother offered, "but on Halloween, my sisters and I would get a mirror and gaze into it as we walked backward down the stairs to the cellar. If we saw the reflection of a man in the mirror, he would be the man we'd marry."

"Did you see Mr. Winslow?" Grace asked

"I don't think it works at all," Mother laughed. "I never saw anyone in the mirror."

"Let's try it!" Grace said.

Thank goodness. Grace seemed like she was having fun.

I got my mirror.

Leaving Tiny and the grownups behind, we piled down the stairs to the back of the store. Dad had drawn the shades on the windows, but light still glowed through the glass in the back door. Grace went first. Holding onto the banister and stepping backwards, she was just about to the bottom step when George popped up behind her and said, "Boo!"

Grace screamed. "George! It doesn't work like that!" She stuck her tongue out at her brother.

George laughed. "Your turn, Josie."

"You . . . " Grace bossed, "stand away from the door and the stairs so you can't cause trouble."

Grace handed me the mirror. "Don't drop it. If it breaks, that's seven years of bad luck."

I held on tight to the mirror and the banister. As I backed down the stairs, all I could see in the reflection was the window of the door and my father making faces at me from inside. Still holding the mirror up, I turned toward Grace. "All I can see is—" My heart stopped. There was a face in the reflection! I screamed and dropped the mirror. Someone ran out from the shadows behind me.

George hollered, "Hey! What the heck?"

"It was Billy Detwiler!" I gasped as he disappeared into the darkness.

Dad came out to see what was wrong.

"Should we chase him?" George asked.

"You can't," Grace said. "We have to be home by nine o'clock, and I'm not getting in trouble again like we did."

Quickly I changed the subject. "The mirror!" I cried.

It lay on the ground next to Grace. She picked it up and turned it over. "Phew! That's lucky," she said. "Still in one piece."

Thank goodness! Not broken. In the darkness something white caught my eye. I picked up a pillowcase and a bar of soap. I looked at the back window where Billy had been hiding. "Daddy, Billy soaped the window." And I wondered if he had tried to break in. But what would he want? The gun was already stolen.

Dad asked, "What's in the pillowcase?"

I peeked inside. "Eggs, matches, firecrackers.

"Some future husband!" George said.

"EEEUWWW!" Grace and I cried at the same time, not at all amused with George's humor.

CHAPTER TWENTY-FOUR

CAN IT BE TRUE?

Finally! Grace and I were back in school. As Miss Penny read aloud after recess, I felt sleepy. The next thing I knew the *whoot! whoooooot!* of a factory whistle woke me. Tolling church bells joined the shrieks of whistles drifting across the river from New Brunswick. I perked up. The clock said two. *Why would bells and whistles be making this racket now?*

Principal Springfield was in the hall. Students ran out of the building despite Miss Morrison shouting for the children to walk. The principal appeared at our door. "It's over! The war is over!"

Cheering, we exploded out of our seats.

"Go on home, children, and celebrate!" the principal called over the noise. "The war is over! School's out for today!"

Books and homework forgotten, we bolted out the door.

Grace and I darted across Second Avenue and rounded the corner for home. The store was packed. Gram and Mother poured sodas and dished ice cream. Everyone talked and laughed at once. Dad took pictures with his Brownie camera.

My father scooped me up and spun around. "It's over, Josie! The war's over!" When he put me down, he said, "Who wants ice cream?" Dad was so excited he poked his finger in the air and practically shouted, "I know, ice cream sundaes with extra fudge sauce, whipped cream, and maraschino cherries!"

Within minutes George burst into the store. "You should see what they're doing in New Brunswick!" he shouted. "Cars and trucks honking horns, people outside making all sorts of an uproar! Kids are running all over the streets! It's a parade like you have never seen!"

Parade? I loved parades. And there were kids there. Grace and I had already had the flu. People didn't usually catch flu twice in the same year.

Grace stared at me, her ice cream spoon stopped in mid-air. "What are you thinking, Josie Winslow?"

"I wish we could go see the parade."

Grace's eyes lit up.

George grabbed the spoon from his sister's hand. "If you're not eating this, I will."

She grabbed it back. "Would it be all right?" Grace whispered. "Maybe if George went with us."

Was Grace coming out of her dumps? For a second, the recollection of the last time the Gardener kids went to a parade flitted across my memory. Was this a good idea? But the war was over. This was supposed to be a happy day. And didn't Dr. Fagan want Grace to have some fun?

"George, would you take us to the parade?" Grace asked.

He hesitated. "It's pandemonium over there."

Dad was taking more pictures. "Here, Josie, let's get some photographs of you three." He motioned for us to stand together.

I decided to ask. "Daddy, may I please go" — a car horn *ahh-uuu-gahed* in the street — "to New Brunswick with Grace, to the parade? We'll go with George."

Dad cupped his ear and leaned closer. "What?"

May I go to the parade, please?" I pointed at Grace and her brother.

"All right," Dad said, handing me the camera. "Get some good pictures. Remember to keep close together." I couldn't believe my father said yes. And he gave me the camera!

After checking with Grace's parents, we hopped, skipped, and jumped our way across the Albany Street Bridge and into a sea of people and noise.

"Let's go up Livingston Avenue, toward the high school," George said.

Mobs covered the sidewalks and spilled into the streets. Men threw their hats in the air. There was hugging. Even kissing! Children banged pots and pans until the metal dented. Flags draped open-air trucks overflowing with people who yelled and waved anything they could get their hands on.

And then there were the fireworks. Everywhere. *Fizzle. Pop-pop! BANG!*

Parade music got louder as the Rutgers band turned onto Livingston Avenue. People of all ages joined the throng of college students marching across New Brunswick. The crowd swarmed around us. Someone jostled my arm, and I nearly dropped the camera. Suddenly George was gone. A man pushed between Grace and me. I grabbed for Grace's hand, but she was just out of reach. Grace tried to get back through the crowd, but she kept drifting away with the tide. Again I tried to move closer to Grace but had no luck.

"Meet me at the library!" I yelled, but I had no idea if Grace heard.

The crowd closed around me, lifting my feet off the ground. I felt like a leaf in a stream. I couldn't see over anybody, let alone see Grace. Briefly, my feet touched the ground. *I've got to get out of here!* Bodies in back pushed me into bodies in front. A cowbell clanged in my ear, and my face got squashed tight against someone's coat. The smell of mothballs and old sweat made me gag. I couldn't breathe. *How will I get out of here?*

Someone grabbed my hand. "Hang on, Josie."

Billy Detwiler? He yanked my free arm. I dropped the camera and reached down to get it.

"Forget the camera!" Billy cried, pulling harder. "You'll get trampled!"

I thought my arm would come out of its socket, but I held onto Billy for dear life.

Billy cursed and bullied his way through the crowd, pulling me along as if he were a lifeguard dragging me out of the Raritan. I found myself on the front steps of the church across from the library.

This couldn't be happening. Billy Detwiler, my personal archenemy, the boy who might have stolen the gun from my father's store, had maybe just saved my life.

"Now we're even," he said.

"Even?" My heart beat fast.

"You helped my mother."

Did Billy actually appreciate what I had done? It seemed impossible.

I scanned the crowd for Grace and George. But even from the church steps I couldn't see over the mass of moving people.

"You were really stupid to get in all this mess." Billy scowled.

"Oh, I suppose it's all right for you to be here because you're a boy. Besides, we came with George."

"A lot of good that did you." He gave me a half-disgusted look.

"Do you see Grace or George?" I asked.

"I'm not looking for them. You're lucky I happened to see you."

Lucky? When has Billy Detwiler ever meant good luck for me?

Billy kept watching the crowd.

I stood on tiptoes to see. Nothing but hats and flags. I was thinking I'd get a better view if I were on the library steps across the street when Billy shouted, *"Scheist!"* He jumped off the steps and pulled a bicycle from the shrubbery. His book bag hung from the handlebars as he hopped on the bike and took off down the side street.

What set Billy off? I turned. Two boys on bicycles barreled past me, and without slowing down, they turned the corner after Billy. The Mackenzies.

I ran to see if Billy got away. Two blocks down the street he glanced back to see if he was being followed. At that moment a car came around the corner. Billy's bike swerved. Dust blew up from the street as both car and bike skidded on cinders. Billy slid sideways under the car. I clapped my hands over my mouth and shut my eyes.

When I opened them, the Mackenzies were pulling at Billy's book bag. A man got out of the car, and the troublemakers disappeared around the corner.

I raced to help Billy. When I got to the car, I could hardly breathe and started coughing.

"Oh! *Mein Gott!* Billy, are you hurt?" The driver of the car bent over Billy. It was Mr. Horowitz. He wrung his hands. "It happened so fast. *Mein Gott!* I didn't see you! Are you all right? Is anything broken? I'm so sorry. I didn't see you."

As I caught my breath, I could see the back wheel of the bike was wedged under a tire and Billy looked pale. Beads of perspiration glistened on his forehead, and bits of cinder and dirt were embedded in his face.

Billy groaned. "I think it's my shoulder or my arm."

"You need a doctor," I panted. "Or the hospital—"

"Josie! *Vhat* are you doing here?" Mr. Horowitz exclaimed.

Billy fussed and tried to get up. "I don't want to go to the hospital."

"Hold still," I said, "in case something's broken."

"Let me take you to the hospital," the baker said, "or at least take you home."

I thought Billy would argue, but he didn't. He seemed to be looking behind me, so I glanced back and saw the Mackenzies lurking around the corner.

Mr. Horowitz helped Billy stand, and I took the book bag.

Billy grabbed for the bag and lost his balance.

"*Vhoa*," said Mr. Horowitz in his thick Austrian accent. "Take it easy. You do not *vant* to hurt yourself more."

"Josie, give it to me," Billy demanded.

"Why?" I asked. "What's so important?"

But then I knew. The gun.

Mr. Horowitz steered Billy to the car, and I hung onto the book bag while I moved the mangled bicycle out of the street.

From the car Billy said, "Josie, give me the book bag. Those Mackenzie boys will chase you."

"Who is going to chase whom?" Mr. Horowitz asked.

I checked over my shoulder. Once more the Mackenzies ducked behind the building.

"Who are those kids hiding around the corner?" the baker asked.

"The Mackenzie brothers," Billy said. "And if Josie keeps my book bag, she will be in trouble with them."

"Get in," Mr. Horowitz said to me. "I *vill* take you both home."

In two short blocks we were back at the corner at Livingston Avenue. I could see Grace waiting on the library steps.

"Mr. Horowitz!" I shouted. "Please—stop! I see Grace at the library. I need to catch up with her."

"Okay, Josie." Mr. Horowitz gently nosed the car through the crowd to the curb. "There is room. I *vill* take you all home."

Before I could get out of the car, Billy grabbed the book bag with his good arm. Hiding what he was doing from Mr. Horowitz, he pulled a dirty rag out of the bag and quickly unwrapped a handgun.

"Is that—" I started to ask.

Billy shushed me.

"Is it loaded?" I whispered.

"No." He kept his head down and shoved the gun into his coat pocket. "We used all the bullets shooting old bottles and couldn't get more." Billy listened to see if Mr. Horowitz had noticed. "There's no time to explain." He pushed the book bag at me. "Leave the book bag on the library steps, but make it look like you're trying to hide it. If those thugs are watching, they'll go for the bag and leave you alone." Billy pushed the book bag at me again. "Go on!"

"Everything all right back there?" Mr. Horowitz asked. "I can take Grace home too."

"Yes, thank you, Mr. Horowitz," I said as I opened the car door. "I'll walk home with Grace. Besides, we need to find George. He'll be worried if he can't find us."

"You are sure?" Mr. Horowitz asked, looking back at me.

But before I could answer, Billy pushed me out of the car, and I stumbled onto the grass. He yanked the car door shut with a bang.

"I'm sure! Thank you!" I yelled so Mr. Horowitz could hear me. The car inched away from the curb back into the crowd.

"Holy cow!" Grace helped me get up. "Was that Billy? Why do you have his book bag?"

"Billy has my dad's gun with him." I held up the book bag. "We have to hide this."

Grace's jaw dropped.

Before I could explain I spied the Mackenzie brothers at the corner.

"Run!" I hollered, and we sprinted to the safety of the library steps.

I made a big show of shoving the book bag behind a pillar in front of the library like Billy said. The Mackenzies disappeared into the crowds.

As we stood on the library steps, I couldn't help thinking that once my parents knew Billy had the gun, Billy would be in trouble. A lot of trouble. Exactly what I had wanted—wasn't it? But he pulled me out of the crowd. He may have saved my life. And he warned me not to take the book bag.

"Josie," said Grace, pulling at my coat. "Are you listening? Do you want to go home?"

"What?" I snapped out of what I was thinking. "What about George?"

"He's right there." Grace pointed at her brother jogging across the library lawn.

As we headed home Grace gave George all the details about Billy. I hadn't heard her talk that much in weeks.

When Grace got to the part about the Mackenzies, George stopped and grabbed her arm. "You don't want to fool with them! They're *real* trouble. For crying out loud, Gracie, they'd steal milk from kittens! Frank told me the older one got kicked out of high school last year and had to go to reform school."

My clothes felt damp, like I had been perspiring. *Maybe Billy knew what he was talking about when he warned me about the Mackenzies.*

Walking through New Brunswick was slow going. Church bells still rang out from every block. We saw a man carrying a stuffed dummy of Kaiser Wilhelm on a pole. People jeered and booed as the raggedy, overstuffed effigy was carried down the street. A gang of children chanted, "Two, four, six, eight, it's the Kaiser that we hate!" Then they threw talcum powder at us.

"Oh! That's just ducky," George groused, brushing powder off his face.

When we got to Albany Street, traffic was at a standstill. Mr. Horowitz's automobile had only gotten this far in the snarl of cars, trucks, and people. To my amazement, Billy jumped out of the car.

Mr. Horowitz leaped out after him. "Stop! *Vhat* are you doing?" He threw his hands in the air in frustration.

Billy headed for the bridge.

"Uh-oh." George pointed up Albany Street. "It's them!"

As long as the Mackenzies were in the crowd, Billy had a chance. But once they got to the bridge, things thinned out and the Mackenzies on their bicycles would overtake Billy in no time. We wriggled through the crowd as fast as we could. Billy stopped halfway across the bridge and bent over with his hands on his knees. He must have been winded. If he didn't get moving, the Mackenzies would catch him for sure. *Run, Billy!*

We ran, but the Mackenzie brothers zipped by and got to Billy first.

George dashed ahead and tried to pull the boys off.

"Leave him be!" I panted as Grace and I reached the tangle of fighting boys.

Grace yelled, "Stop it! Can't you see he's already hurt?"

"Shut up, girlie," one Mackenzie barked as he struggled with George.

"Don't talk to my sister like that!" George jerked that Mackenzie away.

Billy was on the cement. The other Mackenzie held Billy by the shirt collar and stuck his fist in Billy's face. "Where's the stinking gun?"

"In the book bag," Billy said.

"Liar!"

"Stop!" I cried, crouching down to help Billy.

"Take the gun," Billy whispered. "Throw it in the river."

The older Mackenzie pushed me out of the way and grabbed Billy's coat. George pulled him off, and the gun clattered onto the pavement. The boys dove for the gun and sent it skittering out of reach.

"Kick it!" Billy yelled. "Hard! Like you kicked me!"

Never touch the gun. My father's words seared in my brain.

"Now, Josie!" George shouted.

I kicked the gun away from the boys. It slid under the iron railings and into the Raritan. No one would have the gun now.

"Damn it!" The older Mackenzie glared and raised his hand at me.

Grace pulled me close, and George stepped between us and the infuriated boy.

"Was ist los?" It was Mr. Horowitz. He must have followed Billy.

"If you hoodlums know *vhat's* good for you, you'll get out of here right now," the baker warned. "You should be arrested."

"Go back to Germany, you old goat," the younger Mackenzie snarled.

"Shut up," his brother snapped. "Let's go." They took off on their bicycles for New Brunswick, but not without a heap of curses and threats at us.

For the second time today, Mr. Horowitz and I were helping an injured Billy Detwiler. Billy's collarbone now stuck out through the skin and blood seeped into his clothes. Billy moaned, and his eyes rolled back in his head in a dead faint.

"Get my dad!"

George ran the three blocks to the store. Billy came to but didn't know where he was.

"Stay still, Billy," I said. "Help is coming." I tucked my coat around him.

When Dad arrived, he taped bandages on the wound and wrapped gauze tape around Billy's chest and shoulder to keep it immobile. "We're going to take you to Dr. Fagan's," Dad said to Billy. "You'll be all right."

"Mr. Winslow, I want to tell you—" Billy said.

"It can wait, son." Dad put his arm around Billy and helped him to his feet.

"I *vill* drive you," Mr. Horowitz said, as he and Dad put Billy in the car.

"Josie, go home," Dad said, getting into the car with Billy. "Grace, your mother is waiting for you."

When Grace and I walked into the store, customers became quiet. George held an ice bag on his eye where he had been clobbered. Grace's mother spun around on the swivel stool at the counter. "Are you all right?" she asked, coming over to hug Grace and me. "Josie, George was telling us how Billy pulled you from the crowd."

Thank goodness. They're thinking about Billy, not me or Grace. I explained how we'd become caught in the crowd and how Billy saved me. I told about the Mackenzie brothers and the accident.

"It sounds like Billy did you a good turn—" Gram said.

But Mother interrupted. "Where's your coat? There's still influenza around, and here you have been running around with no coat. You'll relapse."

I tried to tell my mother I had only just given the coat to Billy, but she bundled me to the back of the store.

As I passed by the Gardeners, I heard Mrs. Gardener tell Grace and George it was time to go home.

Away from customers, Mother undid the barrette holding the bow in my hair. "You are a mess. How did this happen?"

I explained how we tried to save Billy from the Mackenzie brothers.

Mother pinched the bridge of her nose and pursed her lips. "So, you have been in some kind of fight on the Albany Street Bridge — to rescue Billy Detwiler?" She grabbed my shoulders. "Over the gun? What were you thinking? Life is not a Ruth Fielding novel where no one gets hurt!"

"I kicked the gun off the bridge so they couldn't get it. Besides, Billy saved me. Wasn't I supposed to help him?" I didn't understand why my mother was upset. "And he was outnumbered and hurt. What else could I do?"

"Get help. That's what you could have done! You took a great risk. Did you know if the gun was loaded?"

"Billy told me they had used all the bullets."

"And you believed him."

"Yes, I believed him. And I don't understand how I was supposed to ignore him when he was in trouble. Isn't that what we do? Help people? Isn't that why we went to war? To put bullies in their place and help the victims?"

"It's not the same thing. You are a girl. You are not a whole country."

Gram poked her head through the door. "Everything all right in here?"

Mother took a deep breath. "We're fine."

Out of the blue, my sister asked, "Is Josie going to be bannistered for touching a gun?"

"Tiny, go out front with your grandmother." Mother turned back to me. "Why did you go to New Brunswick without telling us?"

"What? I did tell you. I asked Dad, and he said yes."

Mother shook her head. "He thought you were asking for the camera."

My heart sank. I would never go to New Brunswick without permission. If Mother is this upset, how angry would my father be?

"And where is the camera?"

My dad's camera. "I dropped it when Billy pulled me from the parade. It's probably wrecked." I wanted to cry. "Mother, I didn't mean to go without permission —"

She felt my forehead and tidied my hair. "You've been perspiring. Take a bath and put on dry clothes. Thank God none of you were hurt. Except Billy. Broken bones mend. We'll talk when your father gets back."

≈

From my bedroom I watched people still dancing in the street. Flags hung out of windows. Horns blared. Firecrackers popped. A few doors away, a Victrola played "Keep the Home Fires Burning." It sounded like a funeral dirge. Today was supposed to be a happy day, maybe one of the happiest days in the whole world. The war was over, and I thought I had done something good. And now my parents thought I went to New Brunswick without asking them. Maybe Tiny's right: I should be banished. I wished I could see Billy riding his bike down Raritan Avenue. That would mean things were normal, and I wouldn't be in hot water with my parents.

≈

Dad came home in time for dinner. He handed me my coat and took off his own. "Can you please hang these up for me, Josie? Thank you."

He sounded so formal it made my heart ache. Was Dad mad because I went to the parade without permission or was he mad about the gun? Or the camera? Or everything?

"We set Billy's collarbone at Doctor Fagan's office," Dad said. "Billy told me how you tried to help

254

him. He told me you were the one who kicked the gun into the river."

"Oh Daddy!" I cried. "I didn't mean to touch the gun, but Billy said it wasn't loaded, and he told me to kick it off the bridge. All I could think about was that those Mackenzie boys shouldn't have it!"

Dad nodded. "Billy said you were awfully brave for a girl."

I was stunned. "He said I was brave?"

"Billy's been a thorn in your side since the beginning of school. Why did you feel you had to help him?" Dad asked.

Again I told the story of how Billy had pulled me from the crowd and how I had lost the camera. I told about the accident and the gun, and how the Mackenzie brothers had chased and beaten Billy. "Daddy, Billy helped me today. He may have saved my life."

"He helped you when you were in trouble. It would take a cold heart not to help him in return. For that I am proud of you." Dad paused. "But if I had realized you were going to the parade, I would have said no. Now I think you can see why."

I sobbed. "I am so sorry! I didn't mean to go to the parade without your permission. I thought you said yes."

"I *hope* you wouldn't go without permission," Dad said. "A camera can be replaced, but you can't." Dad pulled me over to him for a hug. "Billy wanted to tell me something. Do you know what it was?"

I shook my head. "I don't know. Maybe it wasn't Billy's idea to steal the gun. Maybe the McKenzie brothers put him up to it or made Billy help *them* steal the gun."

"Billy's an artful liar," Mother said.

"But when Billy pulled me out of the crowd, he said we were 'even' because of his mother. Maybe he's had a change of heart."

I felt confused. I didn't know what to think. I hated being in trouble. I thought I hated Billy Detwiler. All the things he had said about my family. Ruining my middy blouse. The election. Tricking me while the Mackenzie brothers stole the gun. I probably got the flu at his house because I helped his mother when he wouldn't lift a finger. But he was sick too. Did he steal the gun?

"I'll call the constable in the morning," Dad said.

&

On Friday, we found out yesterday's news of the armistice was a false report due to a transatlantic cable delay. *All that for nothing!* Saturday there was no news of a real armistice. Sunday we prayed the war would end soon. Sunday night came, and still there was no news of peace.

CHAPTER TWENTY-FIVE

CHURCH BELLS RING

Monday, November 11, 1918

"Wake up, Josie." Gram gently shook my shoulder. "Do you hear it? Do you hear the bell?"

It was still dark. "A fire?"

"No," she whispered. "I think it's the Reformed Church. The war might really be over."

"What time is it?"

"After four." Gram opened the window.

Cold air drifted in as we listened. Mother and Dad crept into the room. Tiny stayed fast asleep.

"Are they sure this time?" I whispered.

"I don't think they'd make the same mistake twice, do you?" Gram said.

I stuck my head out the window.

"Be careful, Josie," Dad said as he stuck his head out the window too.

It was cold and very still. The gong of the church bell reverberated in the silence. Stars twinkled overhead. Lights flicked on in Mr. Springfield's house across the street.

"Hush." Mother put her finger to her lips. Another bell tolled. "First Baptist, I bet," she said softly. "Thank God, it's finally over."

Dad and I pulled our heads inside.

"It won't be light for a couple hours," Dad said. "Shall we go back to bed?"

My parents tiptoed back upstairs. Gram started to close the window.

"Can you leave it a little bit open?" I asked. "I want to hear the bells."

I cuddled under my covers and lay there, listening. It's over. I sang the little song in my head. *And we won't be back 'til it's over over there.* Soldiers will be coming back. The army won't need Dad. Thank you, God.

Ahhhh-uuuuu-gahh! A car horn broke the stillness. I must have fallen back asleep. The room had grown lighter. I could make out details of furniture and blankets in the soft gray light. Waiting. Waiting to get up, feeling all tingly with excitement. Church bells persisted in the distance.

Ahhhh-uuuuu-gahh! Ahhhh-uuuuu-gahh!

"I guess it's time," Gram exclaimed. "I'm getting up."

"Gram, doesn't it feel a little like Christmas? You know, the bells, before dawn."

Gram sat with me on my bed. Quietly she pulled the curtain aside to look out the window. "I believe you are right, Josie. It does feel like Christmas. She raised her eyebrows and gave me a mischievous look. "Let's make waffles this morning, just like we do on Christmas."

"Bacon too?"

"Of course."

"Can I help?"

Ahhhh-uuuuu-gahh! The one-car parade heralding the armistice sailed back down Raritan Avenue.

❧

I was putting the breakfast dishes away when Dad came up from the store with the newspaper. "Extra! Extra! Read all about it!" he cried. "It's official! Armistice signed! War over at six this morning!" Dad dropped his newsboy voice. "It says they've been parading in New Brunswick since before dawn. An organized celebration will be later."

Parades. Crowds that could spread germs. Crowds that could sweep you away. Billy Detwiler and the Mackenzie brothers. The gun. Maybe parades weren't so much fun after all.

"Well, this is profound," Dad said. "*The Home News* calls the armistice 'the greatest news the world has known since the crucifixion.'"

Since Jesus died?

Gram stopped scrubbing the frying pan. "Don't they mean the *Resurrection?"*

"Good point!" Dad put the paper on the kitchen table.

Mother said, "Maybe this time we should close the store and see the parade and all. Maybe this really will be the war to end all wars."

"Let's hope," Gram said.

Dad left a note thumbtacked to the store door: "Closed for Kaiser's funeral. Service at First Baptist. Interment on George Street near Van Drusen's Drug Store. Back by four."

At church Mother hugged Mrs. Gardener as we joined Grace in the pew. First Baptist was so crowded men had to stand along the aisles and in the back. When we sang, everyone sang, not just the women and the choir. Grown-ups wept.

As our parents shook hands with Pastor McElroy on the way out of church, I told Grace my family was going to New Brunswick for the official parade.

The pastor must have overheard me because as he shook Mrs. Gardener's hand he said, "Going to the parade? Sounds like just what the doctor ordered."

࿔

Later that afternoon we trooped across the Albany Street Bridge. Dad gave us small American flags to wave.

As we got closer to our usual parade spot in front of Van Drusen's pharmacy, homemade confetti showered us as clerks and office workers threw torn up paper out windows onto the sidewalk. Kids ran by sprinkling tiny paper snowflakes and more talcum powder in the air. Boy Scouts marched down George Street dragging an old cannon. Fred and Tony were in the midst of the Scouts. They ran over to see us.

"Isn't this just a crackerjack?" Fred cried. "Janet and Winnie are in the next block." He pointed as Tony dragged him back into the parade. "Yahoo!" he shouted at the top of his lungs and nearly fell down. Everyone laughed.

I tugged on Dad's arm. "May we go find Winnie and Janet? Billy Detwiler's not around," I said, trying to reassure him.

Our dads eyed each other. "If they only go to the next block?" Dad asked Mr. Gardener.

Grace's father nodded.

"Are you sure it's all right?" I double-checked to see that Dad had heard me. I was not about to get us in the same mess I was in last Thursday.

Grace and I wormed our way through the crowd. In no time I spotted Winnie and Janet.

"Isn't this just the best?" Janet asked.

Winnie started jumping up and down. "The hearses! The hearses! Read the signs!" She read aloud, "'Here lies Wilhelm, the crown prince.'"

I poked Winnie and tried to get her to realize it might make Grace feel awkward, so soon after losing her brother. But then Grace shouted, "'Here lies von Hindenburg!'" She laughed, pointing to the hearse. "And there's a goat on top of that car!"

"How do they keep the poor thing on the car?" I asked.

"I don't know, but no matter, we've got the Kaiser's goat!" Grace grinned.

≈

After the excitement of the armistice, life settled down. The flu was still active, but fewer people came down with it and fewer people died. At school, we overheard Miss Penny telling Miss Morrison that the wedding would be in June and she was thinking of inviting our class to the church. In the store, Dad taught me how to roll pills, and upstairs we made plans for Thanksgiving. Sugar, flour, butter. Pumpkin pie. Apple pie. Could we possibly have *both*? Grace talked more about Frank, and we remembered the good times we had had.

≈

The Saturday before Thanksgiving, Dad had me rolling pills in the back of the store when the shop bell jingled. It sounded like several people had come in at the same time.

Dad stepped into the doorway between the pharmacy and the storefront. "Mrs. Detwiler, how nice to see you up and around."

The pills I was making rolled across the counter. I had to move fast so they wouldn't end up on the floor. Then I crept up behind Dad to see.

Dad went out front and shook hands with Billy's father. "Mr. Detwiler, it's been a long time."

"Now that the war's over, I'm able to come up from Aberdeen for Thanksgiving."

There was an awkward silence.

"We're here today to take care of unfinished business," Mr. Detwiler said politely. "And my wife would like to speak to Josie."

She wants to talk to me?

The Detwilers stood by the post office counter. Billy adjusted his coat over his sling. Mrs. Detwiler held a white box with a red bow on it.

"First my son has something to say to you, Mr. Winslow."

"Wilhelm," Mr. Detwiler prompted sternly, "tell Mr. Winslow."

There was a hesitation. "I took your gun," Billy finally said, looking at the floor. "I apologize."

"Go on," said Mr. Detwiler.

"The Mackenzie boys helped me, but it was all my idea."

"Was that you on Labor Day?" I asked.

Dad shushed me.

Billy nodded. "It was me."

"Why? Why did you need a gun?" I blurted out.

Dad put his hand on my shoulder. "Maybe this isn't the time, Josie."

"Daddy, I have to know." I realized then that all along I needed to know why. I looked at Billy. "Someone could have been shot. It could have been you. Was this all part of the bullying? Is it because you didn't like us?"

"No." He paused. "Yes, well, in the beginning it was easy to pick on you. You have everything. Your father's important. You're smart, even if you are a girl. It was easy because you were too nice."

"But the gun . . . " I said.

"Patrick Mackenzie said I was too chicken to steal it. I guess I wanted to show him."

Mr. Detwiler continued. "I spoke with the constable. He said it's up to you to bring charges against Billy,"

The Detwilers looked so miserable. I felt sorry for them.

"We are embarrassed by our son's behavior and apologize for all the damages and inconvenience we have made for you." Mr. Detwiler slid an envelope across the counter. "I hope you will allow us to make restitution and replace the lost revolver."

Dad said, "Thank you," and shook Mr. Detwiler's hand.

Then Mrs. Detwiler stepped closer to the counter. "I have something to add."

Oh dear. What more could Billy's mother want?

Mrs. Detwiler took a deep breath. We waited. Finally she said, "I too apologize for my son . . . and for myself. I believed he was innocent, but now I know better. Now I know better about a lot of things." She looked at Billy. I couldn't read her expression. Was she mad, disappointed, or both?

Mrs. Detwiler composed herself and gazed at me. "And I want to thank Josie. I haven't been very nice to you, and still you helped me when I was ill and had fallen. My sister and Billy told me all that you did. You were brave to help me, and you were brave to help Billy. Your parents must be so very proud."

I thought she might burst into tears.

"I am so sorry if you caught the flu from me. Thank God you and Clementine are . . . " She hesitated. " . . . well." She placed the huge white box on the counter. "I am grateful for your kindness. Please, open it."

265

"Go ahead, Josie," Mother whispered.

The box was from Macy's in New York City! The large satin bow untied easily. I lifted the lid and unfolded the tissue paper. A blouse. A delicate, white blouse with lace and tucks. "Oh, it's so beautiful —"

"I'm sorry I ruined your blouse," Billy interrupted. He shuffled his feet and made a slight motion with his bad arm. "And thank you for helping me when I was hurt." He sort of smiled.

"You pulled me out of that crowd." I smiled a little too. "I think we're even."

৵

On Thanksgiving Day we thanked God for the end of the war we hoped would end all war. We thanked God for helping us survive the epidemic. And we prayed for Frank, that his soul was in heaven and he was at peace. We prayed for the Gardeners and asked God to give them comfort through their sadness.

As we went around the table, each of us contributing our own special thanksgiving, I bowed my head, but I stared at the delicate trim work on the cuffs of my new blouse. *Maybe Billy Detwiler had learned a lesson.* Maybe we had made our own peace. *Was that enough? Had he changed? Had I changed?*

When it was my turn, I said, "I'm thankful no one was shot with our revolver." Heads nodded in approval, but there was so much more I wanted to say.

Dinner done, Dad asked Mother and Gram to hold off on the dishes. "The war's over, it's getting dark, and I can't wait any longer! Let's light the tree!"

I put my coat on and helped Tiny button hers. Outside the sun had set, leaving a faint blue glow in the twilight. It felt like snow. My family gathered around the spruce tree Dad had planted with the Gardener boys in September.

"Josie, go tell the Gardeners we're ready," Dad said.

Grace and I were back in a flash. George followed.

"Are your mother and father going to join us?" I whispered to Grace.

Grace shook her head. "She said Thanksgiving was hard enough." Grace looked back toward her house. "She didn't think she could make it through a Christmas tree too."

My heart ached. Mr. and Mrs. Gardener stood on their porch, watching. I waved, and Mrs. Gardener waved back.

Dad wired the electrical cords to the battery. "Josie, would you like to do the honors?"

"Let George. He helped you plant it," I said. I almost said Frank. Frank had helped too.

George made the final connection and *snap! Crackle!* Sparks flew and we all jumped. The Christmas tree lights blinked once and then the filaments brightened inside the clear bulbs. It worked! The tree lights twinkled like ice crystals. We oohhed and ahhed, Tiny clapped and Dad cheered.

Mother asked George and Grace if they would like dessert. "We have two kinds of pie."

"Two?" George's eyes lit up, and he disappeared with my family into our apartment. Grace and I stayed with the tree a little longer.

I pulled my coat collar around my ears. "I'm sorry your parents won't come over."

Grace blew warm air on her fingers. "I don't think Mother could eat dessert. She didn't bake any pies," Grace said. "Pie was Frank's favorite."

She linked her arm in my elbow and bent her head against mine.

"I'm glad to have a friend who will stick up for me no matter what," Grace said.

"Of course I would stick up for you," I said. "You're my best friend!"

"No, I mean how you tried to do right by Billy even after all the hateful things he did to you. My dad even said he thought you were loyal and brave." She paused. "But he still thinks we were pretty" — she looked around — "damn stupid to go to a parade on our own again. I'll be in college before my father lets me go to New Brunswick without an adult."

"Hey, you two!" George shouted out the door. "Do you want your dessert? I'm going to eat it if you don't."

"Don't you dare! Grace shouted, and we ran into the house.

❧

Later Thanksgiving night, tucked warmly in my bed, I thought about Frank and Billy. And the flu. And the gun. And I finished my thank you list with God.

EPILOGUE

Dad pressed charges against Billy and the Mackenzie brothers. But on Billy's behalf, my father told the court how Billy had pulled me from the crowd in the false armistice celebrations. Since it was Billy's first offense, the judge was lenient as long as Billy's parents followed through by sending Billy to a military school on Long Island. Mrs. Detwiler's health was never the same, and Billy's parents moved to Long Island to be near Billy and Aunt Gisela. The Mackenzie boys were not as lucky. They spent the next few years getting in and out of trouble and reform school.

The flu epidemic continued well into the winter of 1919. We were fortunate. No one in our family perished.

Dad's outdoor Christmas tree was a rarity. They were usually much grander affairs only seen at Madison Square in New York City or years later, the National Christmas Tree in Washington, D.C. Each year my father added another string of lights as the tree grew, and Parkites would stroll past our store at Christmastime to see it. The lighted tree came to remind me that I needn't be afraid and that, with hope, prayer, and a little courage, we could survive harsh times.

In Josie's Day:

Frequently Asked Questions about Spanish Influenza, The Great War, and Life in 1918

Spanish Influenza

What was the state of medicine and infectious disease in 1918?

In Josie's day, kids didn't have to worry quite as much about disease as her parents would have when they were children. Medicine had made significant advances in the years leading up to 1918. Josie would have been vaccinated against smallpox. Improvements in public sanitation would have helped control fatal diseases like typhoid and cholera. Although there was no vaccine to prevent diphtheria, researchers had developed an antitoxin to fight the illness. Death rates were down for tuberculosis. Thanks to pasteurization of milk, fewer babies died from diarrhea during infancy. Still, measles and polio were a significant health threat, and the antibiotics that would help pneumonia patients would not be available until the 1930s. Influenza was only dangerous to the very young or the very old.

How did Spanish influenza start?

Influenza is a yearly occurrence. Today we call it seasonal flu. So, influenza in the winter and spring of 1918 would not be remarkable. Even flu among soldiers in army camps would not be unusual. Soldiers unwittingly took the disease with them to other army camps on their way to France. They called the flu "three-day fever." Elsewhere the flu became known as Spanish influenza, probably because early reports of influenza came from Spain, which was not censoring newspapers. By August, typically the lowest month for flu cases, influenza in Europe was deadly. Soldiers died from lung failure.

Battle plans on both sides had to be altered because so many men were on sick call. Flu was a new kind of killer.

How fast did the disease spread?

During August of 1918 there were scattered reports of influenza arriving on ships docking in New York Harbor, but officials did not think much of it. As Josie and her family got ready for Labor Day and the start of school, sailors coming back from France fell ill at Boston's Commonwealth Pier. By mid-September flu was epidemic along the Eastern Seaboard, and the United States Public Health Service began issuing advice via newspapers on how to avoid catching influenza and how to treat it. By the beginning of October, Spanish influenza had struck in every state in the nation. The worst weeks were in October and the first week of November. Spanish influenza slowly wound down but continued well into the winter and spring of 1919.

How many people were affected by Spanish influenza and how many died?

Experts think that some twenty-five million Americans had Spanish influenza in the ten months between September 1918 and June of 1919. That works out to one in four Americans stricken with the deadly flu. An estimated 675,000 Americans died. Worldwide estimates of deaths from the flu that year range from twenty million to over one hundred million. It is hard to know the exact numbers because, at the time, doctors were not required to report deaths from influenza (although this would change quickly), and in some places, health authorities were so overwhelmed by the epidemic they couldn't keep up with the paperwork. But big numbers are hard to think about. Maybe the lack of coffins tells the story.

So many people died in September and October of 1918 that in many cities and towns there were not enough coffins to bury the dead and gravediggers could not keep up. In some instances convicts dug graves. In Philadelphia the city morgue could handle thirty-six bodies at one time. During the epidemic several *hundred* bodies were stacked in the morgue's hallways, where the decomposing corpses—neither embalmed nor on ice—waited to create their own health hazard.

Did they have a flu shot like we have today?

Yes, but the vaccination of 1918 did not work specifically against influenza. At the time researchers thought the flu was caused by bacteria, and they were able to make a vaccine, but it only affected a specific pneumonia bacterium. Influenza is caused by a virus, and although the medical community knew there were infectious agents that were smaller than bacteria, they did not know enough yet about the nature of viruses to produce an effective flu vaccine.

Could there be another pandemic? Are we prepared? What "weapons" do we have against flu now?

Influenza pandemics occur when a new, or "novel," form of the influenza virus appears. Typically this happens several times every hundred years. In Josie's lifetime she would have experienced not only the 1918 flu pandemic, but also the Asian Flu in 1957, the Hong Kong Flu in 1968, and a swine flu scare in 1976. The 1976 scare started when soldiers at Fort Dix, New Jersey, came down with a new flu virus. Mysteriously and fortunately, that flu did not get out into the general population, but the disease at Fort Dix, the Camp Dix of our story, brought back fearful memories of the 1918 pandemic.

Today public health officials have plans in place to help control the spread of a future pandemic. Worldwide, governments and organizations like the Centers for Disease Control and Prevention and the World Health Organization work together to watch for potential influenza outbreaks. Their plans include identifying a potential pandemic virus as early as possible, creating a vaccine against the virus, and getting that vaccine into production. Making the vaccine takes time, and the medical community is working on ways to speed up the process to get the vaccine ready in time to protect everyone. In the meantime we have antiviral medications that can stop or slow down viruses once a person is sick. We also have antibiotics that can treat subsequent pneumonia associated with influenza. And yes, some of the precautions used by Josie and her family in 1918 are still worth implementing: Stay home if you have the flu, cover coughs and sneezes, and wash your hands after being in public or around a sick person.

The Great War, also known as World War I

What started the war?

Historians point to the assassination of Austria-Hungary's Archduke Ferdinand in June of 1914 as the spark that touched off World War I. The Duke and his wife were on a state visit to Sarajevo in Serbia, a country under the rule of the Austrian Empire. Serbians wanted independence from Austria-Hungary. Austria blamed the Serbian government for supporting rebel activities and wanted revenge. Because of alliances that were in place, by the end of the first week of August 1914, every major power in Europe had declared war on one another. Germany backed Austria-Hungary. The Russians took up the cause of Serbia. France sided with Russia, causing Germany, under Kaiser Wilhelm II, to declare war on France. To invade France, Germany went through Belgium, a small, neutral country protected by a long-standing treaty. Ironically, Germany had signed that same treaty. The invasion of Belgium brought Great Britain into the war on the side of Belgium and France.

People hoped it would be a short war—four months. The Germans said men would be home before the leaves fell from the trees. But all were wrong. Countries around the world would take sides, and the war would grind on for four deadly years.

How did the United States get into World War I?

The U.S. didn't enter the war for three years. From the beginning America did not want to get involved, but several events pushed America into the war. One was the 1915 sinking of the British passenger ship *Lusitania* by a German submarine. The *Lusitania* went down in less than twenty minutes within sight of the coast of Ireland. Over half of the 1,900 souls on board perished, including more than 120 Americans.

Germany had warned the passengers and the public that the *Lusitania* was sailing into a war zone and could be sunk. Afterwards Germany justified the attack, claiming the ship was armed (which was not true), there were munitions on board (true), and the ship was classed as part of the Royal Navy (also true). But still, sentiment against Germany grew as German submarine warfare continued targeting Allied merchant ships and periodically passenger ships without warning.

When the French ferry *SS Sussex* was torpedoed without warning in the English Channel in 1916, President Wilson threatened to sever diplomatic relations with Germany. Germany did not want America to enter the war and promised not to target passenger ships. Germany also agreed that only merchant ships carrying weapons would be targeted and if sunk, the crew would be allowed to abandon ship before it would be destroyed. But the Sussex Pledge was short-lived. By January 1917, Germany resumed unrestricted submarine attacks in an effort to end the war before America could send troops to Europe.

In that same month, a German telegram pushed the United States into the war. In the Zimmerman Telegram, Germany tried to lure Mexico into declaring war on the United States, thinking this would distract

America and keep her out of the European conflict. British agents alerted the United States to the telegram that promised Mexico it would gain back territory lost to the United States some sixty years earlier in the Mexican War. The telegram became the straw that broke the camel's back. America declared war on Germany April 6, 1917.

Life in 1918 Wartime America

What was the Liberty Loan?

During World War I, the federal government raised money for the war through four Liberty Loan drives. There was a fifth bond drive, called the Victory Loan, after the war ended. All were over-subscribed, meaning the government and the people raised more money than they hoped for. Today's United Sates Government Savings Bonds are an outgrowth of the Liberty Bonds.

Usually bonds were sold for large amounts of money. The minimum Liberty Loan bond was $50 — a fair amount of money in 1918. How could the government encourage everyone to participate? A person with a small income or a young person like Josie could buy a Thrift Stamp for twenty-five cents. Children were encouraged to buy Thrift Stamps at school. The stamps were placed in a "book," known as a Thrift Card. When you had sixteen stamps, or four dollars' worth, you took your Thrift Card to a post office or a bank — or even Winslow's Drug Store because it was a post office branch — paid up to twenty-three cents in cash and received a War Savings Certificate Stamp. If you bought your War Savings Stamp in 1918, by 1923 it would be worth $5.00 ($4.23 + interest) and you could cash in the stamp and get your money.

There were often competitions to sell bonds and thrift stamps. School children and their classes competed with each other. Civic groups and churches competed to see who could raise the most money for the Liberty Loan. The firemen in New Brunswick, New Jersey, had a Thrift Stamp sale in September 1918 and were confident they could surpass the $4,000 mark raised by the New Brunswick Police Department.

How did kids earn money in 1918?

Nineteen eighteen was a time when Progressive reformers were trying to control child labor, particularly for children working in factories and coal mines. One way was to make school compulsory. But kids still worked. Some worked because their families needed the money. Others worked at odd jobs to earn pocket change. Like Josie, children often worked in their parents' businesses. Kids collected bottles to earn the refund money. Ten bottles might earn you ten cents, which would buy two nickel sodas or two Hershey Bars. Kids could earn money running errands, raking leaves, cutting lawns, shoveling snow. Delivering newspapers was a common way for kids to earn money. Josie might have earned a penny a paper. If she delivered twenty-five papers a day, she'd have twenty-five cents. In a week she could earn up to $1.75. In two to three weeks she'd have enough to buy the middy blouse in the story, buy some Thrift Stamps, and pay for ice cream at Van Drusen's Drug Store on the way home from the library.

In 1918 goods and services were much less expensive than they are today. A dress "on sale" for Josie would have been between $1.00 and $3.00. A coat could cost as much as $6.50. Girls' high-cut school shoes could be purchased for under $4.00.

Food and grocery items cost far less than they do today as well. But it was all relative. Wages were lower too. For example, a cup of coffee in Winslow's Drug Store might be a nickel. A caramel macchiato at your favorite donut shop is going to be a couple bucks. A cherry Coke (about eight ounces) was five cents. A small Coke at a fast-food restaurant today could run you a dollar or more. Campbell's soup was ten cents a can. Peanut butter was twenty-five cents for a large jar. Gum came in packages of five sticks for a nickel, but gum was hard to get because most gum was purchased by the government for soldiers and sailors.

What was the Clean Plate Club?

The Clean Plate Club was started in 1917 to help children eat all the food on their plates and not waste it. Food was needed to feed soldiers and starving people in Europe. Because of the war, men who used to farm and raise livestock were now in the military. Farmlands of France and Belgium became battlefields. Horses that once pulled plows and farm wagons now pulled great guns across the same fields. Women, children, and the old did what they could, even pulling plows themselves. With half the workforce in the trenches, there were fewer people to work the farms, so there was not enough food.

Under the direction of Herbert Hoover, the United States Food Administration successfully appealed to Americans' patriotism and our country saved sugar, fats, meat, and wheat to help feed the military and our allies. Like their French sisters, women in America stepped up to keep farms running while soldiers were away. Other folks grew food in small vegetable gardens in their back yards. Children tended gardens at school. Americans on the home front came through, saving 15 percent of our own food to feed those in need.

AFTERWORD

Dear Reader,

This fictional story is loosely based on tales my mother and aunt told me about growing up the daughters of a pharmacist during the Spanish flu epidemic of 1918. My aunt, Josie in the story, delivered medicine on her scooter and on occasion gave the patient the first dose. My mother, Tiny in the story, waved the gun from the post office drawer around the store, for which she got quite a spanking, indeed.

My aunt and my mother, along with their cousin, Genevieve, all had the flu at the same time and were nursed together in the front room of the apartment over the store. My grandmother and Genevieve's mother, my great aunt, also had the flu. Neither my grandfather nor Grandma Jenny seemed to have come down with it. And that raised a question for me. Why not? Certainly they were exposed, especially in a drug store, but how did they manage to survive the dreaded disease? And how did my family members who did fall ill manage to live when so many others didn't?

In researching Spanish influenza, I found two answers in Alfred Crosby's book, *America's Forgotten Pandemic*. Possibly my grandfather and his mother did not catch the flu because they had a lighter case of the flu in the spring of 1918 and had developed some immunity. And how did my grandmother, Aunt Hester, Aunt Juanita, Cousin Genevieve, and my mother survive? Probably it was the home nursing they received. Were there other reasons? We can only guess.

A great deal of this story comes from the front pages of the 1918 *Daily Home News*, the local paper of New Brunswick, New Jersey. The side story about collecting linens for the Red Cross "shower" was true. There was an ad on the front page of the paper placed by my grandparents, telling "Parkites" they could leave sheets and towels at the drug store. That was a particularly delightful find among the newspaper archives.

Dr. Fagan is based on my grandfather's friend, Dr. Frank Merrill. According to the *Home News*, Dr. Merrill was called up for the draft in the midst of the epidemic.

Grace and Winnie are based on real-life friends of my mother's. There was a Gephardt's grocery store on Raritan Avenue in 1918, and today, there is still a Quackenboss Funeral Home in New Brunswick.

Billy Detwiler, his family, and the Mackenzie brothers are all fictional characters I created for the book. Other town folk were fictionalized as well.

My grandfather was an avid Kodak cameraman, and many of the images I created in writing are based on his snapshots.

The story about the Gillespie Shell-Loading Plant exploding is true. I don't know for a fact that my grandfather went to help, but he was a volunteer fireman, so it is likely he did.

My Aunt Juanita graduated from Rutgers University Pharmacy School, Class of 1930, and she worked as a pharmacist in the family store with her father.

Kate Szegda
January 2019

FOR FURTHER READING

These books have been written for children, but adults will like them too.

Spanish Influenza Pandemic of 1918

Getz, David. *Purple Death: The Mysterious Flu of 1918.* New York: Henry Holt & Co., 2000.

Hesse, Karen. *A Time of Angels.* New York: Hyperion, 1996/1997. [Fiction]

Micklos, John Jr. *The 1918 Flu Pandemic: Core Events of a Worldwide Outbreak.* North Mankato, MN: Capstone Press, 2015.

O'Neal, Claire. *The Influenza Pandemic of 1918.* Hockessin,

  Delaware: Mitchell Lane Publishers, 2008.

The War and Life in 1918

Freedman, Russell. *The War to End All Wars: World War I.*

  New York: Clarion Books, 2010.

Hazen, Walter A. *Everyday Life: World War I.* Tucson:

  Good Year Books, 2006.

Levine, Beth Seidel. *When Christmas Comes Again: The

  World War I Diary of Simone Spencer.* New York:

  Scholastic, 2002. [Fiction]

Murphy, Jim. *Truce: The Day the Soldiers Stopped Fighting.*

  New York: Scholastic Press, 2009.

**If you are interested in reading an early girls' series
from 1918, an online search could find the *Ruth
Fielding Series.***

Emerson Alice B. *Ruth Fielding at the War Front.* New

York: Cupples & Leon Co., 1918.

Emerson, Alice B. *Ruth Fielding in the Red Cross.* New

York: Cupples & Leon Co., 1918.

ACKNOWLEDGMENTS

To my family and my friends who have supported me throughout this endeavor, thank you for your patience and continuing support. Thank you for always asking about the book and for graciously listening to my interminable commentary on life in 1918. To my critique group, for kind and honest words of encouragement, thank you. To my instructor and cheerleader, Pegi Dietz Shay, thank you for your nurturing expertise in the early days. To Amy Betz, thank you for your editor's eye and for taking on *Pharmacy Girl*. For Susan Robinson, thank you for your proofreading talents. Thank you to Jeanne Kolva, Joanne Pisciotta, and the Highland Park Historical Society (NJ) for creating the three *Images of America* histories of Highland Park. And thank you to Lois Hoffman for her midwifery skills in helping me bring this book into the world.

ABOUT THE AUTHOR

A Jersey girl by birth, Kate Szegda grew up in small towns: Highland Park and Point Pleasant Beach, New Jersey. As a kid, she played the trumpet and loved riding bikes, ice skating, and reading Nancy Drew mysteries. In high school, she worked on the boardwalk selling penny candy.

After earning a degree in English and education, Kate married her college sweetheart. They have two grown children, and over the years, they've had three Labrador retrievers. Their current lab, Emma, often interrupts Kate's writing to remind her that it is time to play.

As a grown up, Kate taught middle school language arts and loved reading books with her students. Two favorites were Johnny Tremaine and Roll of Thunder, Hear My Cry. Historical fiction. No surprise there. Other favorites were Holes and Charlie and the Chocolate Factory.

Now, with time to pursue her passions, she loves working with student teachers. Kate plays golf and likes to travel. Still a reader of middle grade fiction, she loves an afternoon with a good book. But, for Kate, writing Pharmacy Girl has been the best experience yet. According to Kate, historical research — especially about your own family — is a lot like being a detective, and that, she says, is fun.

What's next? Sharing her writing experiences and her book with you.

Visit Kate's website for stories, pictures, and more.

www.kateszegda.com

Made in United States
Orlando, FL
02 January 2023

28069551R10173